Illustrated

MYTHS AND LEGENDS OF CHINA

Illustrated
MYTHS
&
LEGENDS
of
CHINA

The Ages of
Chaos and Heroes

By Huang Dehai, Xiang Jing and Zhang Dinghao
Translated by Tony Blishen

Better Link Press

On page 1
Mural: *Four Spirits in the Cloud* (detail)
See page **68**.

On pages 2–3
Handscroll: *Gods of the Five Planets and 28 Stellar Mansions* (detail)
See pages **64–66**.

This book is edited and designed by the Editorial Committee of *Cultural China* series

Text: Huang Dehai, Xiang Jing, Zhang Dinghao
Translation: Tony Blishen
Interior Design: Li Jing and Hu Bin (Yuan Yinchang Design Studio)
Cover Design: Wang Wei

Copy Editor: Diane Davies
Editor: Wu Yuezhou
Editorial Director: Zhang Yicong
Academic Consultants: Wu Yigong, Sun Yong, Shi Dawei, Zhao Changping

Senior Consultants: Sun Yong, Wu Ying, Yang Xinci
Managing Director and Publisher: Wang Youbu

ISBN: 978-1-60220-157-6

Address any comments about *Illustrated Myths and Legends of China* to:

Better Link Press
99 Park Ave
New York, NY 10016
USA

or

Shanghai Press and Publishing Development Co., Ltd.
F 7 Donghu Road, Shanghai, China (200031)
Email: comments_betterlinkpress@hotmail.com

Printed in China by Shanghai Donnelley Printing Co., Ltd.

3   5   7   9   10   8   6   4   2

Quanjing provides the images on pages 56, 60, 70 and 128.

CONTENTS

Preface   9

A Ballad of the Beginning   13

The Emergence from Chaos   15

Nüwa Creates Man   19

A Harmony Made in Heaven   26

Repairing the Vault of Heaven   31

Kunlun, the Sacred Mountain   37

Jianmu, Tree of the Ladder to Heaven   47

The Severance of Earth from Heaven   51

Dwelling in Nests   55

The Creation of the Eight Trigrams   57

Observing the Heavenly Symbols to Fix the Calendar   63

Auspicious Dragon and Phoenix   71

Shennong the Flame Emperor   79

Drilling Wood for Fire   88

The Noon Market   91

The Flame Emperor's Daughter   93

Yaoji of Wushan   98

The Bird Jingwei Fills the Ocean   102

The Yellow Emperor Builds a Carriage   104

Leizu Teaches Weaving   106

Cang Jie Invents Writing   113

Linglun Makes Music   116

The Great War against Chiyou   120

The World of Yao and Shun   127

Houyi Eradicates the Four Evil Monsters   131

CONTENTS

Houyi Shoots the Suns   133

Chang'e Flies to the Moon   137

Bogun Receives Orders   142

Stealing the Ever-Growing Soil   145

The Spirit's Journey to the West   149

Asking the Way to Lingshan   155

The Arrival of Yu the Great   157
 Yu the Great in His Own Words I   157
 Yu the Great in His Own Words II: Hills, Rivers and Land   159
 Yu the Great in His Own Words III: Making a Path through the Hills   160
 Yu the Great in His Own Words IV: The Xia People   162
 Yu the Great in His Own Words V: Managing the Water and
  Spreading the Soil   165
 Yu the Great in His Own Words VI: As the Will of the Gods
  Would Have It   168
 Yu the Great in His Own Words VII: A Condemnation of Offensive
  War and Setting up the Tripod Cauldrons   171

Epilogue   175
Dates of the Chinese Dynasties   176

Wine Vessel (*Zun*) Inlaid with a Pattern of Clouds in Gold
Han Dynasty (206 BC–AD 220)
Palace Museum, Taibei

The ancients often made a connection between clouds, immortals and mythical
beasts. All gods and Buddha and mythical monsters were able to ascend the
heavens by way of magic clouds and roam the universe. The cloud pattern
became a very common decoration in the Han Dynasty, symbolizing the magic
of heaven. The orderly clouds fill the whole decorated space, seeming to lead
you into a vague void of mysterious illusion that gives rise to a limitless fantasy.

PREFACE
A DISTANT CONSCIOUSNESS

Chinese mythology has a multitude of arterial branches that have played a part in the education of both family and nation and turned a group of people dwelling with nature into a civilized community conscious of its own identity. The virtues and deeds of the heroic figures of legend such as Pangu, Nüwa, Fuxi, Shennong the Flame Emperor and Yu the Great have been widely acclaimed. Their sense of morality courses unceasingly through the veins of the people, relaying an integrated spiritual model of the Chinese race.

Science has flourished but in the centuries that have elapsed since reason came to dominate the world, things that have remained despite all efforts to remove them, may have done so because they possess some particular strength. Myth and legend, for example, has not disappeared without trace from the modern world, but thrives and spreads in the fields of literature and art. Myth and legend is not a relic of the ancient past but a distant consciousness to which we are closely bound.

There is not a single unfamiliar story in Chinese mythology. These stories are concealed, latent in our living world in simple and definite forms, handed down by word of mouth, growing and multiplying. Our ancestors emerged from chaos, foraged for food in groups, sought out suitable places in which to live, pursued and fought and escaped from wild animals. From their settlements they cautiously crossed rivers, climbed the peaks of mountains and looked out on the four corners of the earth. They made their way through forests into the open spaces. They enjoyed the warmth of the sun, the sound of rain and water and experienced the cold chill of snow and ice. As time passed their limbs grew more adaptable and their minds quicker, encompassing love and hate. They developed from individuals into groups, to city-states and nations and to fresh wars and

Mural from the West Slope of Mogao Cave No. 249 (detail)
Western Wei Dynasty (535–556)
Dunhuang
Dunhuang Academy, Gansu Province

Fengbo and the Rain Master is the god of wind and rain in Chinese mythology. This mural shows King Asura in the center, with four eyes and four arms, standing in the ocean with hands raised, holding the sun and the moon with the sea beneath his feet. Painted above his head are the mountain Sumeru and the heavenly palace of Daoli with its door half open, half shut. Fengbo and Rain Master and others stand at the left of King Asura (see the detail on page 122). The whole has a sense of the interplay of thunder and lightning and the combination of wind with rain.

peace. Poverty gave way to wealth but once material needs were satisfied there remained the cultivation of mind and spirit as well as matters of good and evil, greed and desire and praise and punishment. Every aspect and corner of a culture was encapsulated in the form of a story.

Each generation rewrote the original myths and legends on the basis of the vicissitudes of their own time, thus maintaining the vitality of the legends. The "inner meaning" of a myth lies in the process of birth and rebirth with its tendency towards a perfection of form that occurs continuously in the study of mythology. For instance, at a time when usurpation of authority was common in society, rewritten legends would somehow have something added to them. As an example, the more people were able to climb the "Jianmu, Tree of the Ladder to Heaven" and see the beauty of heaven and hear the stories of the gods, the more they were filled with envy, expecting that they, too, would one day become gods. But familiarity breeds contempt, they came to feel that there was nothing particularly special about the gods and gradually became presumptuous and disrespectful. Inevitably, this brought about the later punitive separation of earth from heaven. The retellings of later generations (and even the audacious rewriting) are part of the process of the constant re-creation of ancient legends. Through this process new meanings and forms are added and thus those seemingly remote myths always maintain their vigor.

The Greek gods of Olympus were not just waiting there to be excavated or dredged up, like a buried cultural object or a sunken ship. It was only with the poets Homer and Hesiod that the genealogy of the gods was established. Similarly, it was only through Virgil and Ovid that the Roman people learned of the sources of their own legends. We can conjecture that the western culture of Greek and Roman legend powerfully expresses the childhood of human society. Nevertheless, the understanding of early Chinese culture on the part of the

Searching the Mountains **(detail)**
Song Dynasty (960–1279)
Anonymous
Ink and color on silk
Height 53.3 cm by length 533 cm
Palace Museum, Beijing

Ever since legends began in prehistoric times, the illustrated images of spirits (*jing*) and monsters (*guai*) have had an extensive influence, almost to the point where they have become the best textual footnotes, as for example the images of spirits and monsters in the *Classic of Mountains and Seas* (*Shanhai Jing*). *Searching the Mountains* is a good example of this genre. The picture depicts the soldiers of the gods led by heavenly generals searching for demons and monsters in the mountain forests where spirits and monsters appear as wild animals, or in their original form, or transformed into women, fleeing in panic from the pursuit of the heavenly generals.

western reader generally extends as far as Confucius and Laozi and no further. An analysis based on the co-ordinates of world culture suggests that the era of Confucius and Laozi equates with the period of the rise of Greek philosophy. The date of the death of Laozi is more or less that of the birth of Socrates and distant less than ten years from the passing of Confucius. In fact, the equal and opposite culture of China has a similarly rich mythological tradition that has nurtured the world imagination and sense of emotional well-being of generations. Through a combination of text and illustration this book seeks to present a succinct yet vivid description of these distant and ancient stories.

The compilation of this book has benefited greatly from the mythological research of an older generation of scholars. We would like to express our gratitude both to Mr. Zhao Changping for his scholarly work on Chinese creation myths and also to Mr. Zhao and his co-authors Mr. Luo Yuming and Mr. Wang Yonghao for their book *Record of Chinese Creation Myths*, an important reference source.

A BALLAD
OF THE BEGINNING

At the beginning of chaos,

There was nothing written.

At the opening of heaven and earth,

Came the songs of the heroes.

Within the four seas,

Spirits and demons beyond number;

Vast in joy,

A myriad legends.

When the nine provinces formed,

Then the beginnings of culture.

Legends of China's creation,

Splendor beyond compare on every page.

THE EMERGENCE FROM CHAOS

In the beginning, heaven and earth existed in chaos and utter darkness covered all. In the limitless dark emptiness was an enormous black egg. The primeval essence known as Pangu grew quietly in this chaos, noiselessly, like the fermentation of a seed before it sprouts, undisturbed, in silent absorption.

In this way, eighteen thousand years passed. Then the primeval essence juddered and chaos seemed to start in fright as, astonishingly, a crack slowly appeared. At first, just fine cracks appeared, spreading very, very slowly. At a time unknown, there was a slight tremor, the cracks opened faster and faster and the sound of cracking changed from light and crisp to ponderously heavy. Then, almost in the twinkling of an eye, chaos split in two, the clear, light portion drifting slowly upwards to become the heavens and the heavy, turbid portion slowly sinking to form the earth. At the same time, like a chick pecking at its shell as it emerges, heaven and earth separated and

Pangu awoke from his slumbers and stretched gently. Seemingly in order to avoid Pangu's stretching, heaven and earth at once moved away, heaven upward and earth downward.

The awakened Pangu was as one with heaven and earth and grew with them. Each day heaven grew higher by a measure, the earth thickened by a measure and each day Pangu grew taller by a measure. But strangest of all, as the heavens grew brighter and the earth more solid, Pangu underwent nine changes in a day, sometimes floating free as a cloud, sometimes rumbling like thunder, sometimes as lofty as a mountain peak, sometimes stretching forth like a river, sometimes as compact as clay, sometimes as gentle as grass and trees, sometimes blazing like the stars, and sometimes as dazzling as a jewel. At other times he crawled like an insect ... wise in spirit, unfathomable in change, surpassing the constantly changing heaven and earth.

In this way there passed another eighteen

Pangu Opens the Heavens
2017
Feng Yuan (1952–)
Ink and wash painting
Height 308 cm by width 198 cm

Legend has it that when Pangu awoke from the lacquer black darkness, he grew larger by night and day in the space between heaven and earth, changing many times each day. Each day heaven grew higher by a measure, the earth thickened by a measure and each day Pangu grew taller by a measure … In this way, ten thousand eight hundred years passed, the heavens reached their utmost height and the earth its utmost thickness. Pangu became a giant whose feet stood on earth and whose head touched the heavens.

On pages 12–13
Four Immortals Offer Birthday Greetings (detail)
Ming Dynasty (1368–1644)
Shang Xi (dates of birth and death unknown)
Ink and color on silk
Height 98.3 cm by width 143.8 cm
Palace Museum, Taibei

Four immortals are crossing the ocean on the waves and look up in greeting at the God of Longevity, the old man of the south pole, as he rides the heavens on the back of a crane. This auspicious picture expresses the common subject of birthday greetings as well as conveying the hopes and prayers of the ancients for a long life. Technically, the brushwork (*bimo*) is delicate and the figures lively in expression, the line is rich in tension.

thousand years, the heavens grew higher and higher and the earth deeper and deeper and between them Pangu stood on earth supporting the heavens, enormous in stature. Between heaven and earth there lay a distance of ninety thousand li (one li equals 500 meters), the very height of Pangu whose girth was immeasurable. On an occasion, standing between heaven and earth, Pangu became weary and drooped a little. Heaven and earth shook, the earth moved upwards and heaven downwards as if closing in towards each other. Pangu roused himself and straightened up, standing again between heaven and earth. When the tremor died away, heaven was at a slant and the earth had become mountainous and uneven. Fearing that the tilted heaven would continue to press down, Pangu once more summoned up his courage and strength and piled up two great mountains and set them between the slanting heaven and earth.

Pangu, the only living creature between heaven and earth was sometimes happy and the skies brightened, sometimes angry and the heavens darkened; sometimes he opened wide his eyes and there were flashes

of lightning; sometimes he shouted with joy and the sound became thunder; sometimes he dripped with sweat and the heavens were filled with rain; sometimes he sighed in relief and his breath turned to gusts of wind; sometimes he wept with loneliness and his tears formed rivers and streams. There were times too, when he dreamed that he had turned into a great dragon, disporting itself in the vast spaces between heaven and earth, a dragon that flew up and up to the heavens where, at first, the sky was bright blue and then a hazy grey and where, higher still, the

Mural from the East Slope of Mogao Cave No. 285 (detail)

Western Wei Dynasty
Dunhuang
Dunhuang Academy, Gansu Province

Nüwa absorbs the essence of Pangu's now underground vitality and gradually assumes physical form. Here, she is one of the two gods that appear in the center of this ceiling mural, either side of the jewel. Both gods have human heads and the bodies of snakes. The stomach of each is painted with a disc of red. They are clad in long-sleeved gowns, wear long head coverings and in their hands hold a rule, a carpenter's set square and an ink marker. A pattern of clouds and flowers is set between them.

colors changed ceaselessly. At this point the startled Pangu always woke from his dreams.

The yin and yang elements of light and dark endlessly succeeded and replaced each other and once more countless ages passed. Even Pangu, who was as old as antiquity itself, grew aged and bent. By this time, fortunately, heaven and earth were more or less stable, and even if Pangu bent a little, they merely trembled slightly and remained unmoved. In the end, Pangu's body came apart, each piece of it separating bit by bit. Pangu's vitality penetrated deep into the earth, his left eye became the sun and his right the moon and his hair and beard became the stars. The hands and feet and torso became the four points of the compass and the well-known mountains of the five directions. His blood turned to rivers and the muscle and veins became paths and roads and the fat and flesh turned to farmland. Teeth and bones became gold and stone, his skin with its hair became grass and trees and the marrow turned to pearl and jade. Little by little, Pangu's dying body took on the shape of the earth, everything in it containing some of his primeval essence, growing vigorously like Pangu himself when he stood between heaven and earth and beginning its own experience of birth, age, illness and death.

After a long, long time, the now underground vitality of Pangu absorbed the essence of heaven and earth, gradually growing and taking on form. A head burst from beneath the ground, first the top and then the skull followed by the features as an enormous human head emerged. At first it looked out blindly and then, as it adapted to the sunlight, the massive skull slowly turned in all directions; its eyes wide open, taking in everything on earth. Immediately, a long, long body came twisting up out of the earth as the surrounding soil collapsed. Then, suddenly, with a shake, something soared into the air where it cruised in space—the body of a serpent!

Yin and Yang

The ancient Chinese, observing the opposite but related natural phenomena that occurred in the world of nature, such as heaven and earth, sun and moon, night and day, hot and cold, man and woman and up and down, placed them in two categories of relative opposites, yin (dark) and yang (light). They used this principle of the duality of change to explain movement and change in the material world.

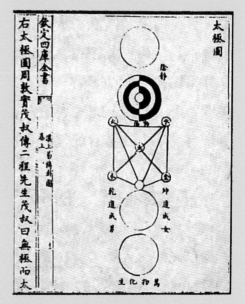

Title Page of *A Cosmological Chart of the Great Ultimate*
A Cosmological Chart of the Great Ultimate is a work by the Song Dynasty philosopher Zhou Dunyi (1017–1073). The text only amounts to 249 characters in all. Inspired by the *Xici* section of the *Book of Changes*, Zhou Dunyi believed that the "Great Ultimate" (*taiji*) was the origin of the universe, man together with all living things was constituted from the mutual interaction of the energies of yin and yang and the five elements of water, fire, wood, metal, and earth. The five elements became united in yin and yang and yin and yang became united in the Great Ultimate.

NÜWA CREATES MAN

This god with the body of a serpent and the head of a man, born of the primeval vitality of Pangu and infused with the essence of heaven and earth, was later called Nüwa. When Nüwa burst forth from the soil, the realm of heaven and earth was still a vast emptiness, immersed in the vapor of desolation, where enormous wild beasts roamed the earth and huge birds hovered in the heavens. The water in the rivers was still and had yet to flow, it was as peaceful as if the water could hear the sound of the sun rising in the east and setting in the west. Now and then, a great fish would leap from the surface and the sound of a resounding splash would shatter the stillness, earth and heaven would brighten for a moment and then return to stillness whilst, one after another, crystal clear

Detail of T-Shaped Painting on Silk on page 20

wavelets rippled across the water.

At first, Nüwa was not lonely, the world was large and she had playmates enough. She could change her form seventy times in the space of a day, one moment into a lion or tiger leading a dance of all the animals; the next as a phoenix joining the birds in song; another time diving into a river and playing with the great dragons. In a storm she changed into a tree standing in the wild and listening to the first sounds of nature. When her curiosity was

T-Shaped Painting on Silk

Western Han Dynasty (206 BC–AD 25)
Length overall 205 cm, width at head 92 cm, lower width 47.7 cm
Hunan Provincial Museum

Excavated in 1972 from Tomb No.1 at the Mawangdui Han site in Changsha. When excavated, the painting lay on the inner coffin of the tomb. Finely executed with fresh colors and fluent line the painting abundantly reflects the style and success of early Han painting. The painting is divided into upper, middle and lower sections, presenting scenes from heaven, mankind and below that embody the thinking about the achievement of immortality through magic of the early Western Han Dynasty.

The section dealing with heaven occupies the most expansive space at the top. At the upper right-hand corner there is a golden bird superimposed upon a red sun. A further eight suns can be seen amidst the Fusang tree beneath. A new, crescent moon, with a toad and jade rabbit above, occupies the top left hand corner. Beneath, Chang'e is shown flying to the moon. Seated between the sun and moon there is the figure of a long-haired heavenly god with a human head and the body of a snake with an all-encompassing long red tail. There are also mystic dragons and birds facing each other in an obvious display of the awe and divinity of heaven. The content of this painting bears a distinct resemblance to the content of many legends, particularly the presence of Chang'e flying to the moon and Houyi shooting the suns. Many scholars believe the seated god of heaven with a human head and snake's body to be Nüwa.

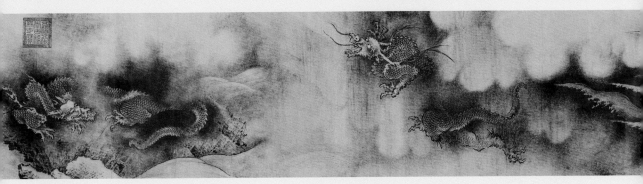

Above

Handscroll: *Nine Dragons* (detail)

Southern Song Dynasty (1127–1279)
Chen Rong (dates of birth and death unknown)
Ink and light color on paper
Height 46.3 cm by length 1096.4 cm
Museum of Fine Arts, Boston

In Chinese culture, it could be said that the dragon is the ultimate totem. Mankind is filled with awe of its mysterious image as it swoops through mist and cloud and soars through the nine heavens, and has embodied it with a spiritual hope that has partnered the development of Chinese culture throughout without any great change. Chen Rong's *Nine Dragons* is a relatively early and valuable example of a dragon picture that depicts the nine dragons swooping and soaring, appearing and disappearing through wind and wave. It presents an overwhelming portrait of the dragon's mysterious powers of infinite transformation.

Below

Handscroll: *One Hundred Birds Attend the Phoenix* (detail)

Qing Dynasty (1644–1911)
Shen Quan (1682–1760)
Ink and color on silk
Height 40 cm by length 1600 cm

The phoenix (*fenghuang*) is the legendary king of all birds. The *feng* and *huang* were originally two birds. The *feng* was male and the *huang* female and phoenixes in flight were a symbol of good fortune and harmony. This scroll depicts close on three hundred birds including ducks, magpies, wild geese, peacocks and the red-crowned crane. The two phoenixes at the heart of this picture are modeled with elegance and dignity and splendidly colored. The tail feathers are meticulously delineated, as is the luxuriance of the leaves and branches of the paulownia tree that bears the two birds. Throughout the length of this scroll, all kinds of birds and trees combine together to form a picture of a colorful, vibrant, intoxicating and vital natural world.

Handscroll: *Nine Dragons* (detail)

aroused she could change into a low-flying insect, wings trembling like a grasshopper, or the croaking of frogs or chirping of cicadas, or even into the beautiful sound itself with the strength to continue without stopping. At that time, the universe was a place in space and time that opened and closed at will. When Nüwa arrived, time and space opened and all living things joyfully appeared for her; when she left, time and space closed and the world and time both returned to a desolate wilderness.

Time flies and Nüwa, having changed into almost everything on earth that grew, or moved, or flew or swam, found her high spirits and enthusiasm weakening; there were times when there was nothing that she wished to change into. She just roamed the heavens dragging her long body behind her. It felt as if there was something in her heart that she needed to say, something that she needed to do, but was unable to express to all around her. In her loneliness, Nüwa felt the desolation of the world and thought that there was something lacking. She now often paused on the riverbank, lost in contemplation of her image upside down in the water. One day a myriad shoal of fish passed by in the river and disturbed her reflection. Watching the reflection shivering in the water as it gathered and then dispersed, her mind was numb and her heart heavy. It was as if some earth-

Handscroll: *One Hundred Birds Attend the Phoenix* (detail)

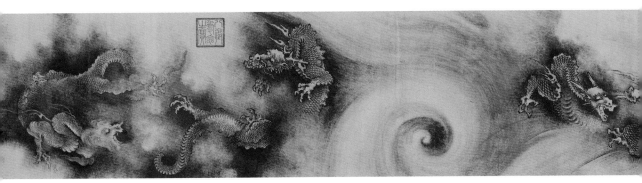

shattering event was about to occur but she had no idea of what it might be.

Nüwa descended the bank and gathered a handful of fine yellow earth, added water and began to knead it vigorously. Slowly the earth began to take on a shape. With continued kneading the earth displayed the features of a face and the seven openings of a head that resembled Nüwa herself. Looking at the earth as it gradually took shape, Nüwa seemed encouraged and her hands kneaded faster, forming a body with arms. When she reached the lower half of the body, Nüwa looked back at her own tail and, recalling the monkeys leaping in the forest, made two legs like theirs but thicker. After she had pinched out two feet larger than a monkey's, she set down the human form that she had kneaded and smiled at it. The manikin created from the fine yellow earth was in every way lifelike but Nüwa still felt that it lacked something. Knitting her brow, Nüwa thought for a while, comprehended and then directed a long breath into the manikin's nostrils. Once she had expelled this breath, Nüwa felt her mind clear and her heart lighten. She looked up and saw to her surprise that the tiny manikin she had kneaded from earth had been transformed into a body of flesh and blood. It had come to life and was happily skipping away into the distance, chirping the while.

Handscroll: *Nine Dragons* (detail)

Nüwa gained great joy from the process of turning earth into a person, the loneliness in her heart eased and looking at the first manikin as it made off into the distance she enthusiastically created another. When she had completed her kneading she breathed on it and the figure of mud came to life and ran off into the distance, the sound of its merry laughter returning to her ears. Nüwa's enthusiasm increased by leaps and bounds and she began to use her left and right hands to knead separately, breathing when she had finished. Something strange now happened. Originally, the figures created by kneading with both hands together had combined yin and yang in a single body. However, using left and right hands to knead separately, produced, surprisingly, male and female, the left with its yang responses producing men and the right with its yin responses producing women. They would surround Nüwa for half a day watching her make mud figures, some would even speak with her and then turn and chatter unintelligibly together before happily rushing off into the distance.

After having kneaded for she knew not how long, Nüwa grew weary, but none of the figures she had made at first had stayed with her, they had all gone far away. Nüwa came to realize that the newly created children would not stay with her forever and would always leave, it was just that in this age of desolation

Handscroll: *One Hundred Birds Attend the Phoenix* (detail)

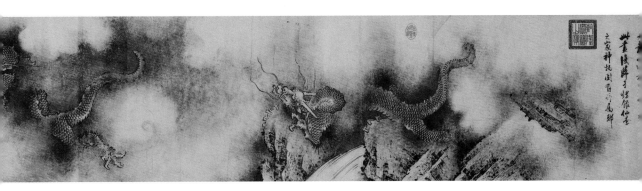

the present children were obviously too isolated. There really needed to be more of them. But Nüwa's strength would soon be exhausted and she must think of a solution. She suddenly had a brainwave. She went up into the hills and fetched a length of rattan that she then dipped into the river and stirred about. Very quickly mud and water combined to form a sticky paste. Nüwa waved this mud-coated rattan in the air whilst at the same time breathing on the droplets that it scattered. Once the droplets of mud fell to earth they turned into a joyous crowd of people. The humans produced by this spatter from the rattan, although slightly smaller than those produced by kneading, were in no way different in wisdom. Nüwa became happier and ceaselessly waved her rattan, spattering the ground so that it was soon covered with traces of humanity.

Now, Nüwa who had labored for so long stopped. She gazed at the people far and near and, as weariness overtook her, she felt the kind of peace that follows fatigue. Nüwa slept and in her dreams saw the people that she had created all weaving plants and trees together to form dwellings as they began a life of bustle and excitement. Suddenly, deep in her happy dreams, Nüwa's heart sank, she seemed to have forgotten something important and was obliged to wake from her slumbers and stare fixedly into the distance.

A HARMONY MADE IN HEAVEN

When mankind was first created no place had a name and men wandered the limitless wilds of nothingness. The world produced enough and man did not need to work; he reached up and plucked fruit from the tree when he was hungry; when he was thirsty he lowered his head and drank from the river; when he was tired he sought out a cave or a hollow in a tree and lay down to rest. Sometimes, when the mood took him, he would cut open a ripened gourd and float in it on the river at his pleasure; sometimes, when the hills were covered in snow, he would fell a dead tree and use it to go up and down the mountain.

Now and then, as she watched her children, who seemed without a care in the world, Nüwa forgot that vague something in her dream, she sensed what was in their minds and enjoyed the all-pervading mood of happiness. Until, one day, she saw a child fall from the mountain into a bottomless abyss, and watched its playmates burst into tears of sorrow. She watched the crying children with a heavy heart and their weeping only ceased when she went down to the riverbank, molded another child and placed it amongst them. Afterwards, Nüwa knitted her brow and that vague but important matter suddenly raised its head. She realized that her creations would grow old and decrepit and would die and that it was impossible for her to go on making manikins like this forever. She now knew what she had to do.

The next day, Nüwa made a reeded *sheng*, an instrument shaped like the tail feathers of a phoenix with thirteen reeded pipes inserted into half a gourd, each pipe connecting to a mysterious world. She played alone in a leisurely way and the children who had been larking about sensed that some anxiety of their own was being addressed, quickly lost interest in playing, abandoned what they were doing and slowly gathered round her. Both male and female phoenix, *feng* and *huang*, heard the sound of the *sheng* and flew to circle above Nüwa, male and female intermingled, their necks entwined; dragons flying abroad heard it and danced high in the clouds, facing each other in pairs around a beautiful dragon pearl; four-legged animals heard it and each in their herds pursued the other; the great fish heard it and carrying their eggs within them bounded from the surface of the water to fall back with a crash; grass and trees heard it and opened huge flowers casting their pollen into the air; the stones heard it and from east and west returned a distant echo.

As night approached, the mountains blocked out the sun. In a spot struck by lightning, trees and vegetation burned, the light from the flames reddening the sky and the faces of the people. They had heard the sound of the *sheng*, their hearts trembled, and the redness of face caused by the fire burned into their senses. They began to dance with abandon, holding hands, stamping the ground, coming together, declining, smiling, exchanging embraces, intoxicated with the rhythms of the body and oblivious of all else. Once the dancing finished, the joyous men and women understood all and with flushed faces made their way into the depths of the forest hand-in-hand with their partner of choice. The moon and stars of the sky became their canopy and a mattress of grass their bed.

Gold Filigree Hairpin Inlaid with Emerald Green in the Form of Two Dragons Playing with a Pearl

Qing Dynasty, Qianlong period (1736–1795)
Palace Museum, Taibei

From the beginning of the Western Han Dynasty the "two dragons playing with a pearl" motif became an auspicious decorative design used mostly on the household utensils and ornaments of the nobility, imparting an air of vigorous grandeur to the whole. The illustration depicts a hairpin of the Qianlong period when the dragon motif was frequently used and of finer work than that of later dynasties.

Modest girls shielded their faces with fans plaited from bulrushes. Amidst the melodious sound of Nüwa's *sheng* playing, the rivers flowed strongly, trees suddenly grew tall, the dew formed damp on the blossoming flowers and their marriage was consummated. This blessing from Nüwa, a marriage observed by heaven and earth, was called "A Harmony Made in Heaven."

Ten months after this wild party came the bawling of infants as earth received its first babies. These infants could not be allowed to be soaked by the rain or left in the wind. They could not eat the same as adults or be allowed near the hot breath of wild animals, their tender bodies seemed sensitive to everything. Suddenly, the adults became busy and, like birds, built nests in the trees. They began to draw water and chop firewood and to cook food over a fire. They used the feathers and fur of birds and animals to cover their young. The young became more and more numerous and very soon all that the earth produced was not enough. Nüwa planted seeds in the earth

On facing page
Detail of *One Hundred Birds Attend the Phoenix* on pages 21–25

A Palace Music Party (detail)

Tang Dynasty (618–907)
Anonymous
Ink and color on silk
Height 48.7 cm by width 69.5 cm
Palace Museum, Taibei

This picture depicts twelve ladies and others of the palace harem seated round a square table, relaxing with music. The gracefully elegant ladies are tasting tea or playing forfeit drinking games. The four in the center are adding to the merriment by playing wind music. The one on the extreme left is holding a *sheng*, a kind of reeded panpipe. One of the two standing maidservants is beating out the rhythm with a pair of clappers. The atmosphere is one of great sophistication.

and the earth grew plants that could be eaten. Man began to till the soil and learned from Nüwa how to grow plants. From then on mankind began to increase in number and to begin a labor of its own as over first one, then two and then three generations, the seed of mankind spread across the earth.

Nüwa had created and given life to man and shown it, through example, how to increase and spread. By teaching it about cultivation she had instructed mankind in work and now she felt that she could truly rest from her labors.

REPAIRING THE VAULT OF HEAVEN

For generation upon generation, mankind flourished and spread and the earth was bathed in tranquility. Man knew awe and stood in awe of water and fire, the hills and forests, pathways and directions, and even of mountain caves and their nooks and crannies. This sense of awe grew over the long years to become the gods of heaven and the spirits of earth. In the beginning there was no form to these gods and spirits, just a disembodied energy drifting in the heavens. Later, this disembodied energy gradually coalesced and gave form to the gods and spirits. By the time that Nüwa was in her old age, there were gods and spirits almost everywhere throughout the world.

At first, the gods and spirits lived in peace, each secure in its own position, enjoying the reverence of those of mankind that belonged to them. But there was continuous change, the sense of awe in mankind blazed forth and the form of the gods expanded, then grew weaker and began to shrink. Gradually, differences of size appeared amongst the

Nüwa Repairing the Vault of Heaven

Qing Dynasty
Ren Yi (1840–1895)
Ink and color on paper
Height 118 cm by width 66 cm
Xu Beihong Memorial Hall

In its depiction of the solidity of rock, this work reflects the resolute determination of Nüwa as she repairs the vault of heaven.

Ren Yi was an outstanding modern artist whose all-embracing technical skills included *shanshui* (landscapes), birds-and-flowers, and figure paintings.

gods and spirits. After an accumulation of countless years, the gods and spirits of fire and water became the two biggest. Originally, Gonggong the water god had been the biggest and because man frolicked in the rivers and lakes and was able to eat their fish and prawns most of his awe was reserved for the water god. But after the birth of generation upon generation of children, mankind became accustomed to cooking food and Zhurong the god of fire became more and more important, his body growing larger and larger. When Zhurong's body reached more or less the same size as that of Gonggong the latter became angry and resentful.

Unable to suppress his increasing anger Gonggong challenged Zhurong. There was a great battle, the two huge gods fought from heaven to earth and back again and as time passed it seemed impossible to distinguish the victor. But because of increasing reverence from mankind, the longer the battle lasted the more Zhurong's body grew and his strength slowly overtook that of Gonggong so that victory was only a matter of time. Finally, Gonggong was defeated and with his anger unassuaged he turned against one of the two great mountains erected by Pangu and struck it in two. The upper half fell and shook the earth. Because the mountain was no longer whole it was later known as the Less-than-Whole Mountain (*buzhou shan*).

Long accustomed to the support of this great mountain, heaven and earth now fell into a violent tremor. With the collapse of the

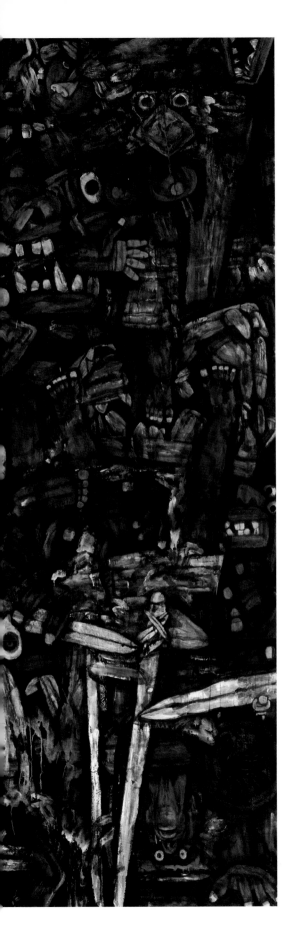

mountain a great rift appeared in the heavens through which the rain came bucketing down. Apart from the great tremor caused by the fall of the mountain, cracks without number also appeared, the earth began to tilt and lava flowed from beneath its surface as fires spread through mountain and forest. Because the earth had tipped, the hitherto undisturbed rivers and lakes overflowed their banks and spread across the vastness of the world. Birds and beasts and the fierce dragons in the great rivers were terrified and began to attack each other and sometimes humanity as well, so that many perished in these disasters. In her peaceful old age, Nüwa's heart ached at the disasters that had befallen her children. But these gods and spirits were the creations of her own children, she could not perish in their stead, she had to bring this catastrophe to an end in her own way.

Nüwa collected a great many stones of seven different colors from the rivers and lakes. She put them in a large furnace and smelted them into a colored glue-like liquid. She was already tired as she did this but she knew that she had to finish the task before her. She rested a little beside the furnace and then flew to the high heavens carrying the refined liquid with her. Where the heavens had collapsed the rain stabbed her painfully

Gonggong Turns His Wrath against the Less-than-Whole Mountain

2017
Shi Dawei (1950–)
Ink and washing painting
Height 430 cm by width 400 cm

The water god Gonggong, who controlled the floods, engaged in a great battle with Zhurong the god of fire and was defeated. He thereupon turned his wrath against the Less-than-Whole Mountain, one of the pillars of heaven, and struck it a blow that cut it in two. Half the sky then collapsed leaving a hole through which the rain poured in torrents, flooding the world. Only when Nüwa had manufactured stone of many colors and repaired the vault of heaven did the world return to normal.

like so many sharpened knives. Paying no heed, Nüwa flew on towards the opening and bit by bit, using the glue made from the stones she repaired the cracks in the vault of heaven. The rain lessened, the heavens were complete again and a curtain once more covered the earth. Because of the different colored stones that Nüwa had used the heavens now shone with a light that became the seven colors. We can see these seven colors shining from the rainbow after rain has fallen.

When Nüwa returned the earth was still in chaos. The underground lava and the water from the lakes and rivers had kept her children in the midst of deep water and fierce flames. The exhausted Nüwa summoned up her remaining strength and dived into the largest lake, seized its biggest turtle and used its four limbs to set between heaven and earth to form the four pillars of the sky. The earth shook once more and then slowly settled, the fires gradually went out, the floods receded from the four corners of the

Hornless Dragon (*Chi*)

The *chi* is an ancient legendary animal. One version has it that it is a kind of sea monster, another that it is the second of the nine sons of the dragon.

In Chinese folklore the *chi* dragon stands for beauty and good fortune. The *chi* pattern is also one of the classic patterns of traditional Chinese decoration, first found on the bronzes of the Shang (1600–1046 BC) and Zhou (1046–256 BC) dynasties. It is also found in ancient Chinese architecture, domestic buildings, porcelain, jade and personal ornaments.

earth and the world once more appeared in its familiar and well-loved form. Nevertheless, mankind was still most troubled by all the ferocious things that flew or swam or moved or grew. Yet again the utterly exhausted Nüwa summoned her remaining strength and killed

Detail of *Nine Dragons* on pages 21–25

the Black Dragon in command. Following Nüwa's example, mankind began to rid itself of the wild beasts and ferocious birds in their own way. Thus, after the passage of very many years, the earth was at last restored to tranquility.

But, however well the vault of heaven had been repaired, there were still cracks, so that the heavens inclined to the northwest and the sun, moon and stars all moved in that direction. The sun moved the fastest and the stars the slowest; the earth itself inclined to the southeast so that the rivers flowed eastwards and the place where all this water converged later became the sea. From this time forward there were the four seasons and night and day. Hot and cold weather took over from each other, the sun rose and set, and mankind began to live in joy and in peace with the animal kingdom so that newborn babies could be placed in the nests of birds to be rocked by the wind as if cradled by nature. This was truly the

Hornless Dragon (*Chi*) and Grain Pattern Disc

Diameter 20.4 cm, diameter of circular aperture 5.8 cm, thickness 2.0 cm
Color: blue-green with signs of ageing, some staining
Ming court jade
Palace Museum, Beijing

The center aperture is decorated with a carved dragon and the surface and outer edge of the disc are decorated with eight hornless dragons in high relief. The other surface is decorated with an incised grain pattern, all with the meaning of "the hope of success for a child" (*jiaozi chenglong*). A grain pattern on one side with hornless dragons in relief on the other is a characteristic of Ming and Qing jade discs. This is probably a ceremonial jade.

golden age of mankind. But Nüwa was indeed old and, mounting her dragon-driven thunder chariot and preceded by a hornless dragon (*chi*) and followed by a flying serpent, she flew up and up to the very heights of heaven. Mankind watched sadly as Nüwa flew far away and disappeared over the distant horizon.

KUNLUN, THE SACRED MOUNTAIN

After Nüwa had repaired the vault of heaven, mankind entered a period of untrammeled ease and leisure. In truth, it was an unsurpassed golden age. Were it possible, everybody would have sought to hold onto this stretch of time as a gift in perpetuity. Alas, there is nothing in this world that can be held back, beauty and sadness both pass by, we cannot halt time just as we cannot prevent water from flowing. In the end, time must pass, we should be in no hurry to hasten towards the next period of suffering, let us

Gold Inlaid Boshan Burner (detail)

Western Han Dynasty
Overall height 26 cm, diameter of foot 9.7 cm
Hebei Museum

Boshan burners are also known as Boshan incense burners and are a commonly encountered type of Han and Jin (265–420) dynasties vessel for burning incense. They are mostly made of bronze or pottery. The body of the burner reflects the 豆 (*dou*) chalice shape of ancient bronzes. There is a tall conical reticulated lid shaped like an undulating mountain carved with birds and beasts symbolizing Boshan, the mythological fairy mountain in the sea from which the burner takes its name. (It was widely believed during the Han Dynasty that there were three fairy mountains in the sea—Penglai, Boshan, and Yingzhou.)

The gold inlay on the burner outlines in gold thread and strip a pattern of billowing clouds. The upper body and lid bear a cast pattern of undulating hills. The mountainous reticulations of the lid present a lifelike sculpted scenery of hills in which mythical beasts come and go and leopards and tigers dash about. Nimble monkeys squat on the upper peaks or ride playfully on the backs of animals, whilst amongst the hills hunters armed with bow and arrow go in search of prey.

just pause here for the moment.

At the time, heaven and earth had long resumed their good humor and the sun, moon and stars rose in the east and set in the west in their accustomed place and accustomed order. The rivers flowed gently and steadily eastwards; there was dawn mist and evening cloud. Usually the world was bathed in warm sunlight, moose and deer ran in herds, peacocks spread their tails, the great beasts crouched and lay, finches gathered and flew while gigantic trees shaded the leaping monkeys and squirrels as the wild grasses flourished and then withered through summer heat and winter cold. At the time there was neither ferocity nor aggression amongst men, carelessly twisting a tiger's tail or stepping on a poisonous snake met with no ill consequences. Man took everything in his stride, life was long, and he was neither burned by fire nor drowned in water. He could walk the heavens as on earth and clouds could not obstruct his vision or thunder disturb his hearing. Man used knotted string to record events, happy in his own customs, secure in his dwellings, setting forth without thought of destination, cheerfully munching food at play and patting his belly as he wandered abroad. Man went to sleep at ease and woke naturally, even sometimes treating himself as if he were a horse. He did not dream and woke without anxiety. In eating there was no distinction between coarse and fine or sweet and bitter and he breathed with the longest of breaths.

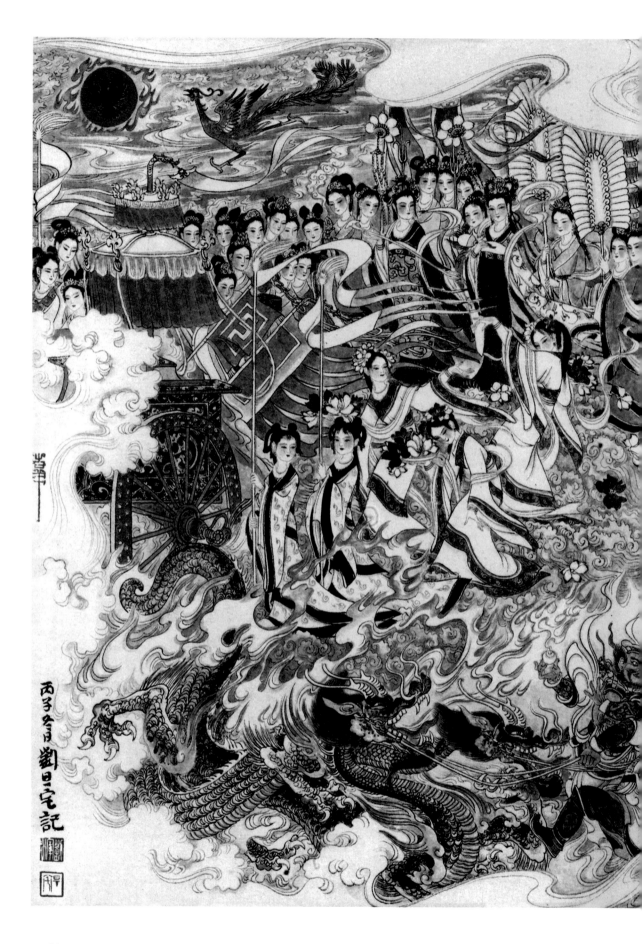

When the people rejoiced they stamped their feet and with animals' tails in their hands performed different kinds of music, sometimes "nurturing the people," sometimes "cultivating grasses and trees," sometimes "venerating the principle of heaven," sometimes "establishing the accomplishments of the sovereign," sometimes "relying on earth's virtues" and sometimes "establishing the ultimate of birds and beasts"[1]. This music sang the praises of the earth that had brought forth mankind, or celebrated the luxuriant growth of grass and trees, or expressed reverence for nature or hope for an understanding of the Emperor of

1 Translator's note: These titles are from the Ph.D thesis *Analysis of the Discourse on Music of the Lushi Chunqiu* by Jo, Jung Eun, SOAS, London 2012.

On previous spreads

Lamentations

1974
Liu Danzhai (1931–2011)
Ink and wash painting
Height 38 cm by width 60 cm

Lamentations (*Li Sao*) is a literary work by the poet Qu Yuan (c. 340–c. 278 BC) of the Warring States Period (475–221 BC). The painting borrows lines from the poem and depicts the flight of the poet's imagination in the realm of fantasy, from the Cangwu hills in the south in the early morning to the vast panoramas of the Kunlun Mountain of the northwest in the evening.

There is a contrast in the construction of the picture between right and left and solidity and emptiness, the floating elegance of line suggests a feeling of splendor, while the hero Qu Yuan stands grandly with the sleeves of his robe floating in the breeze as the immortals approach the world.

Left

Forty Views of the Old Summer Palace— Pengdao Yaotai

Ink and color on silk
Height 64 cm by width 65 cm
National Library of France

This album contains forty leaves depicting the forty individual scenic settings in the greatest palace garden of all, the Old Summer Palace (Yuanming Yuan Garden). The paintings of buildings, streams and rocks are finely executed in the realistic manner.

This leaf is a representation of the Pengdao Yaotai (Jade Terrace of Paradise Island). The view comprises three islands and its structure and composition are based upon the "one pool three hills" principles of artistic design and construction of the Tang Dynasty painter Li Sixun (651–716). The three hills are the legendary immortal mountains of Penglai, Fangzhang, and Yingzhou. At the time, when standards of production capability were low, mankind was powerless to subjugate nature but expressed its worship of nature through myths and fairy tales. The Kunlun legend symbolizes the worship of mountains and the legend of Penglai is symbolic of worship of the ocean. The fairy tale palace parks of the Chinese imperial house were born of the legend system derived from this worship of nature.

Heaven, or respect for the ordering of events according to the mood of the four seasons or an expectation of the ultimate in birds and beasts. As man performed this music so the secret doors of heaven and earth opened one by one and the especial sounds of heaven and the pipes of earth mingled with the music of man. Thereupon, all earth's living things together with mankind itself were immersed in this flow of music as every vein and hair on every leaf opened in joy.

Sometimes, humans recalled Nüwa who had created them and looked up towards the high Kunlun Mountain in the distant west. When Pangu set up two mountains to settle the shaking earth, one had been the Less-than-Whole Mountain broken in two by Gonggong and the other had continued to stand, towering over the furthest reaches of the west and because it appeared vague and indistinct (*hunlun*) it became known as the Kunlun Mountain. There was nothing that compared in height with the Kunlun Mountain, layer upon layer and fold upon fold it edged ever upwards to a height of eleven thousand *li*, one hundred and fourteen paces, two *chi* (one *chi* equals 0.33 meters) and six *cun* (one *cun* equals 0.033 meters). The mountain is surrounded on all sides by the Weak Water Abyss where the water is so weak that even a feather cast upon it sinks immediately. The foot of the mountain is encircled by a great hill that emits fire and flame and from this volcano there grows an ever-burning tree, the wind cannot make it burn more fiercely nor the rain put it out. The birds and beasts, trees and shrubs on this mountain of flame rely upon fire for their existence. On the mountain there is a rat weighing upward of one thousand *jin* (one *jin* equals 0.5 kg), with fur two *chi* long whose whole body glows red in the fire but turns as white as snow as soon as it leaves. When its fine silken fur becomes dirty it merely has to pass through the fire once for it to become as good as new again. Later, when man had learned the art of weaving, this fur was shorn and woven into cloth that when dirty was heated in a fire and at once cleansed. This cloth was known as "fire-washed cloth" (*huohuan bu*).

At the time it was believed that Nüwa, who had left the world in her thunder-chariot, lived in the uppermost heavens and sometimes visited the mid-mountain by way of the Kunlun Mountain peak. The mid-mountain was called Cool Wind Hill and formed a barrier against the flame and fire of the mountain foot that allowed a climate suitable for humans to exist in the mid-mountain. Man believed that from the hill ranges of the mid-mountain Nüwa often observed

Long Life and Never Grow Old (*Changsheng Bulao*)

Originally a Daoist phrase meaning life in perpetuity without aging. Like Confucianism, Daoism is an indigenous Chinese religion. The central tenets of Daoism include belief in Laozi as its founder, denial of the mandate of heaven and of the Buddhist law of the consequences of actions and resistance to the laws of nature in the search for perpetual youth, as well as the use of written spells to cast out evil spirits.

Colored Enamel Porcelain Birthday Bowl with *Lingzhi* Fungus and Crane
Qing Dynasty, Yongzheng period (1723–1735)
Palace Museum, Taibei

This delicate, finely bodied bowl is painted with the *lingzhi* fungus, the red-crowned crane and the paradise flycatcher bird (*shoudainiao*—seal cord bird) to express the concept of the "birthday greetings of immortality." From ancient times the *lingzhi* fungus has been regarded as a symbol of good fortune and long life under the name of "the grass of immortality." The red-crowned crane is also a metaphoric representation of a long and prosperous life. The paradise flycatcher bird has two very long central tail feathers, rather resembling the cord (*shou*) attached to a seal and elegant in appearance. Moreover, *shou* (cord) is a homophone of the character *shou* meaning long life and thus bears the same metaphoric meaning. Historically, these three have been traditional symbols of prosperity and long life.

The Eight Immortals Greet the God of Longevity (detail)

Song Dynasty
Silk tapestry
Height 41.3 cm by width 23.8 cm
Palace Museum, Taibei

Heads raised, the Eight Immortals clasp their hands in greeting as they watch the God of Longevity arriving from the heavens riding on the back of a crane. The God of Longevity is the spirit of long life of ancient legend. The Eight Immortals are eight Daoist immortals widely known in traditional Chinese folklore. "Eight Immortals Offer Birthday Congratulations" is a frequent popular celebratory subject often seen in embroidery, porcelain and on the stage.

This tapestry, woven from colored thread on a plain ground, contains numerous figures within a very small space. Even so, the attitudes and actions of the Eight Immortals are naturally and realistically portrayed. The facial expressions are lively and the differing characteristics of the immortals are strongly brought out. Beards and eyebrows shown by stitches and taken with the realistically animated facial features present an example of exquisitely delicate needlework.

the humanity that she had created from afar. Further up the mountain from Cool Wind Hill there was a garden. The garden was looked after by a god called Yingzhao who had the body of a horse with stripes like a tiger, the wings of a bird and the face of a man. The garden was already a long way up and seemed suspended in space so that people called it the "Hanging Orchard." A rivulet of sweet water flowed round the garden and was called Sweetwater Spring. Beneath the Hanging Orchard there was another spring of clean, clear bone-chilling water called Jade Water, which flowed directly into the Emerald Lake. The view upwards from the Hanging Orchard encompassed all the wonders of heaven whilst all the vitality of mankind was spread below for all to clearly see.

At the summit of the Kunlun Mountain there grew a rice seed four *zhang* (one *zhang* equals 3.33 meters) high and of a girth that encompassed the length of the arms of five men surrounded by countless stands of barley growing round it. To its west grew trees of pearl, jade of two kinds, and trees of everlasting life; to the east there were Shatang trees and trees of tinkling gems from which grew jade like pearls that were the food of heavenly birds. A six-eyed beast called a Lizhu, each of whose three heads slept in turn, guarded the trees of tinkling gems both day and night. The eyesight of the Lizhu was good, it could see the new growth of hairs on bird and beast in autumn and so nothing could draw close to the trees. South of the great rice seed there were the purple Jiang trees where eagles, poisonous snakes and Shirou, the seeing flesh lived. Once a piece of Shirou's flesh was eaten another piece grew in its place and it recovered its original appearance. It could never be eaten up. Later, was it possible that the cassia trees in the Moon

Palace that could never be cut down were Shirou in another form? To the north of the great rice seed lay trees of all kinds of jade and gems that blossomed with pearls and jewels.

Man firmly believed that he had only to go to the Kunlun Mountain and set foot on Cool Wind Hill and he would live forever; enter the magic Hanging Orchard and he would acquire supernatural powers; climb on from the Hanging Orchard to the summit of the Kunlun Mountain and he would become a god and dwell there with Nüwa. This was a beautiful and boundless hope and prayer that held within it a sense of aspiration and longing. But amidst all this beauty a great disaster was brewing and was approaching mankind step by step.

On facing page
Vase with Nine Peaches
Porcelain painted with colored enamels over a transparent glaze
Height 51.1 cm
Qing Dynasty, Qianlong period
Metropolitan Museum of Art, New York

This is a vase of the Qianlong era when much auspicious decoration drew on metaphors of the natural world. It was an era characterized by delicacy of painting, clarity of arrangement and luxuriance of content.

There is an overall decoration of a peach tree with a sturdy trunk and branches bearing the nine peaches. A Chinese rose climbs in contrast alongside. Legend has it that the Queen Mother of the West (*Xiwangmu*) lived in the sacred Kunlun Mountain. Her garden was planted with the peaches of longevity which only flowered and bore fruit once every three thousand years and when eaten increased longevity. When the peaches ripened the Queen Mother of the West called the immortals together for a great birthday banquet. As a result, the peach pattern has become a traditional symbol of longevity.

Above
Auspicious Cranes (detail)
Northern Song Dynasty (960–1127)
Zhao Ji (1082–1135)
Height 51 cm by width 138.2 cm
Ink and color on silk
Liaoning Provincial Museum

The ancient Chinese believed that the crane was the sacred bird of immortality. In this painting Zhao Ji, the Song emperor Huizong, has used a representation of "magical clouds and auspicious cranes" as a metaphor for good fortune and blessings.

The hand scroll depicts a palace roof complete with its wooden bracketing standing against a sky filled with rosy clouds. Eighteen red-crowned cranes circle above, each in a different attitude, while another pair perch at the very top of the roof. The whole atmosphere of stately solemnity conveys a mysterious air of good fortune. The picture is densely colored and the technique exquisite.

Emperor Huizong was the last emperor of the Northern Song Dynasty. He excelled in painting and calligraphy and possessed considerable artistic talent.

JIANMU, TREE OF THE LADDER TO HEAVEN

Man had but to climb to the very top of Kunlun to be able to change from a human to a god and to enjoy the immortality denied to mankind forever. But strange to relate, despite the knowledge that, in those days, man could walk in the air, no one had ever heard of an ordinary mortal reaching the summit of Kunlun. It was gods, immortals and wizards who could travel between heaven and earth by way of Kunlun. Consequently, although there was a shortcut to immortality through Kunlun, nobody had ever actually achieved immortality that way.

There had been those, reluctant to give up, who had attempted to fly across the Weak Water Abyss and over the Flaming Mountain and who, if they had not been almost drowned, had been scorched by the flames and had retired in embarrassment. Nothing in the world remains forever and later when

The Sky Ladder Tree
2017
Li Chaohua (1958–)
Oil
Height 200 cm by width 160 cm

The sky ladder tree in the middle of heaven and earth is a bridge joining the men of earth with the gods in heaven. The mythologies of the peoples of China contain many similar sky ladder legends. The Miao people, for example, have a legend that "the giant redwood is a sky ladder to the myriad heavens." The legends of the Dulong people of Yunnan state that between heaven and earth there are huge numbers of terraces from which mankind can ascend to the heavens; the Oroqen people bury their dead in trees believing that trees are a medium through which people may ascend to heaven after death.

man's desire to fly to the top of Kunlun had faded, the many mysteries of Kunlun were gradually scattered to be seen no more and Kunlun became one of the world's mountains.

It is the way of mankind that the more something is beyond reach, the more strongly it is sought after. Particularly by those first creations of Nüwa that combined yin and yang in one body. By the time the mysteries of Kunlun had faded, they were already ancient and more and more recalled cherished memories of the capacity to climb Kunlun to become a god. They hankered after the ability to reach heaven and achieve immortality and searched the world to find a ladder that would reach it. At the time, there were many legends of such ladders. There was an immortal called Bogao from east of Qingshui, Mount Hua who had climbed to heaven from there, and there were wizards at Mount Dengbao in the wilderness of the west who had climbed up and down from heaven. However, these were just stories circulating at the time, nobody had seen it with their own eyes. Nobody, let alone the figures in the stories, whether immortal or wizard, had heard of ordinary people reaching heaven by way of a mountain.

Nüwa's first creations were far too conceited and, of course, were not prepared to give up merely on this account. They carried on searching for a ladder. They very soon thought of the different kinds of tall trees. They had visited the great wilderness where there was a great red tree whose evergreen leaves bloomed with scarlet flowers that reflected red on the ground; they had been to the wilds of Ousi where there was a triple trunked mulberry tree, several hundred measures high that never grew leaves; they had been to the south of the ancient country of Juying in the north where a great tree grew beside a river, its trunk reaching into the clouds, its leaves spreading a thousand *li* and shading the four points of the compass; they had been to the country of the People of Black Teeth, where, in the place where the sun rose, a Fusang tree with a circumference of two thousand girths grew to a height of two thousand *zhang*. Clambering to the tops of these trees they were close to heaven and seemed to be able to reach out and pluck the stars from the sky. But

Sacred Tree of Bronze

Height of damaged trunk 359 cm, overall height 396 cm
c. 1700–c. 1200 BC
Sanxingdui Museum, Sichuan Province

From the Sanxingdui archaeological site at Guanghan in Sichuan Province. This large bronze sacred tree comprises base, tree, and dragon. It is the largest Bronze Age structure so far discovered in China.

The base of this bronze tree is modeled on the concept of three interlinked hills making up a "magic mountain." The tree is cast as the very center of the "magic mountain peak" with direct access to the heavens. The tree itself is divided into three layers, with each layer comprising three branches, nine branches in all; on each branch there are two fruit stems, one upright, one hanging, a bird stands on each upright stem. In all, there are twenty-seven stems of fruit on the tree as a whole and nine birds. A bronze dragon climbs down the side of the tree.

Scholars believe that the Sanxingdui sacred tree of bronze must be a kind of combination of the mythological Fusang and sky ladder trees, one of its principal functions being the ability to "connect with heaven," linking gods with men. In this way, gods and spirits may descend to earth and shamans ascend the heavens, the dragon may climb the tree and the shamans ride it.

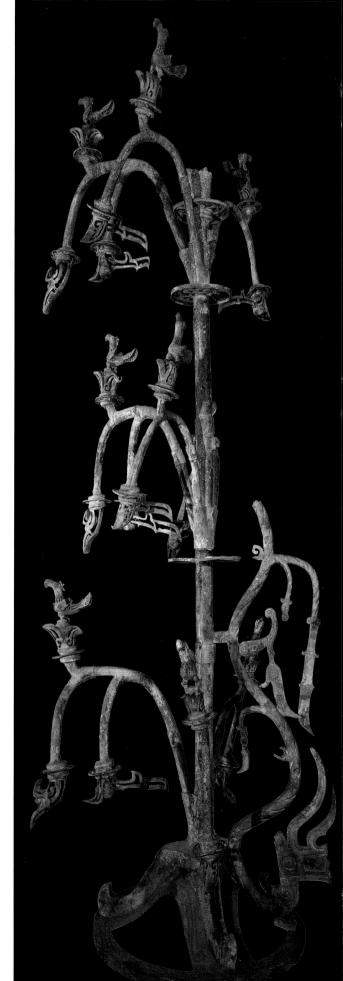

it was impossible to climb into the heavens by way of these trees; when almost there that apparent proximity became an unclimbable distance.

Later, these discontented people finally reached the wilds of Douguang. It was said that this was the center of the world, trees and grass remained green through winter and summer and all kinds of seed sprouted as soon as they fell to earth. The seeds were smooth and white, rather like fat. Birds hovered and four-legged animals gathered. Surrounded by all sorts of plants and animals there was a kind of tree called the "soul of long life," which stretched out, branch by branch, until it disappeared into the distance. Any branch broken from the tree could be used as a staff for the elderly without further treatment. The long life tree was right in the middle of the wilds of Douguang where a tree known as Jianmu grew. This tree was at the center of heaven and earth and every day at noon its shadow disappeared. If you stood beside the tree and shouted, it was if something breathed in the sound, there was no echo at all. There were no branches to the sky ladder tree, just a long slender trunk that penetrated the sky. At its very top there grew a curved branch that coiled like a dragon into a canopy like an umbrella. The branches of the tree appeared a deep purple color and the leaves were a gleaming blue-green and shaped like thorns, the blossoms were great black flowers and the fruit was yellow in color like hemp. If you pulled at the tree the bark came

Stone Relief: *The Phoenix Holding a Pearl in its Beak and the Winged Tiger Offering an Object*

The image of a phoenix holding a pearl in its beak frequently appears alongside people in the stone relief of the Han Dynasty. The pearl is the elixir of immortality given to the person in the portrait by the phoenix, thus expressing the yearnings of the people of the Han Dynasty for long life and immortality.

off and the purple turned yellow, the delicate bark resembling a tasseled ribbon, like a yellow snake.

In fact, in finding this tree mankind had found its own path to heaven and many of the yin-yang bodied people had climbed up, using the tree as a ladder, and had enjoyed a brief period of happiness in heaven. However, they had not really become gods as in the legends. Moreover, their conceit had led to a series of incidents that had aroused the wrath of the gods who had pulled down Jianmu and destroyed the ladder, completely severing man's route to heaven. Before we tell this tragic tale, let us pause again for a while, and consider the secret warnings that the gods had given early on.

The great god Taihao was the first to use Jianmu for passage between heaven and earth. Taihao was the great emperor of the east; his assistant was Goumang the wood god. Goumang had the head of a man and the body of a bird, his face was square and he was often dressed in white and traveled abroad driving two dragons. He carried an imaginary disc that he could make bigger or smaller, with which he could test the accuracy of the seasons and assist Taihao in the governance of spring. Goumang's original name had been Chong and when, in spring, trees and grass appeared, twisted and curved, the wood god who controlled spring became known as Goumang. The peculiar Goumang seemed to have been a forewarning, constantly reminding people that although it was right to have the spirit to grow upwards, in fact such growth upwards should twist and turn and take a roundabout path. Bypassing all the difficult sections and going straight up was, in the end, to meet huge obstacles and even to bring great disaster upon oneself. Mankind, in using Jianmu to reach heaven, seemed to have lacked a certain circuitous prudence and incurred punishment thereby.

Stone Relief: *Goumang, the God of Spring*

Eastern Han Dynasty (25–220)
Shaanxi History Museum

Excavated in 1996 from No.11 tomb at the Han tomb complex at Dabaodangzhen in Shenmu County in Shaanxi Province. In the folklore mythology of ancient China, Goumang is both the god of woods and of spring, exercising dominion over the growth of trees and plants and of agricultural production as well. According to the *Classic of Mountains and Seas*, Goumang had "the body of a bird and the face of a man," just like, as it so happens, the figure on this stone relief.

THE SEVERANCE OF
EARTH FROM HEAVEN

We must remember that when Nüwa created man it was by no means the essence of heaven and earth that was obtained but yellow earth from the riverbank. Fortunately, Nüwa had breathed on mankind who had then received an original essence as pure as that of Nüwa and Pangu. But yellow earth was, in itself, a product of man, carrying with it the mud and stink of earth. Consequently it was difficult for the human body to avoid smelling of mud. Before finding Jianmu, mankind had kept within its own limits and had not envied anything of the gods, nor had it thought to change into a god and was thus able to maintain the purity of its original essence and live in the world free of care. As more and more people climbed Jianmu to heaven and saw its beauty and heard the stories of the various gods, they were filled with envy and hoped that, one day, they too could become gods. At the same time, familiarity bred contempt, they felt that the gods were nothing in particular and gradually became disrespectful. Especially towards the Great Central Emperor, whom they felt was far too nice and benevolent an old man who sometimes displayed uncouth behavior which did not accord at all with his position.

This not knowing when enough was enough on the part of mankind eventually roused the malignant deity, Chiyou. Chiyou had originally been a minor god, to whom people dedicated their occasional evil thoughts. However, as people's dissatisfaction with the Great Central Emperor became increasingly apparent, Chiyou's evil-mindedness grew and grew and from a minor god he gradually turned into a major god. When he believed that his strength was sufficient, he climbed down Jianmu and went amongst the people inciting a rebellion of an alliance of the nine tribes. Not only did he incite rebellion, he sought by all means to force people to follow him, punishing the virtuous and rewarding the evil. Malice was encouraged, the stink of mud and earth from the bodies of humanity grew strong and spread and the goodwill that came with the original essence was utterly suppressed, while Chiyou himself grew even more enormous. Evil took encouragement from itself and soon spread throughout the world. When he believed that he was strong enough to defeat the Great Central Emperor, Chiyou lead a band of people up Jianmu to Heaven to wage war and overturn the established order.

When the normally amiable and benevolent Great Central Emperor was confronted by this evilly intentioned invading army, his characteristic warmth changed suddenly to a terrible severity. With thunderous fury he battled with the evenly matched Chiyou and eventually, with the help of Xuannu, the Dark Lady, defeated him and destroyed the humans who had followed him up the tree into heaven. When they came to understand the wrath of the Great Central Emperor, people did not thereby increase their respect for him but felt, rather, that he had been too severe and was too remote. In the words of Confucius "distance breeds complaint," he was not fit to enjoy their goodwill. However, those able to reckon the odds became quick witted and acquired more respect for the craftier gods. This cast of mind accumulated over countless years and produced Zhuanxu, a resourceful master of stratagem. Wearied of mankind by this fierce battle and after many years of the silent education and minute observation of Zhuanxu, the Great Central Emperor gradually diminished and retired, leaving the governance of the affairs of heaven and earth to him.

The day Zhuanxu, who "conceived stratagem in solitude and acquired knowledge abroad" gained power, his first act was to separate those who combined yin and yang in one body into two. He cancelled man's ability to fly and ordered the Thunder God to fell Jianmu that allowed gods and men to travel between heaven and earth. He sent Chong and Li to cut off all possible routes between heaven and earth. Chong is the wood god previously called Goumang and Li is the fire god previously called Zhurong. These two gods had originally harbored deep goodwill towards mankind. Zhurong had defeated the reckless water god Gonggong and long before disaster occurred, Chong, in his own image, had warned mankind to be vigilant and not to conceive any ideas of usurpation. Now, however, the mood of the populace had changed and it had no patience with hints delivered in secret. The two gods, therefore, had no alternative but to meet the demands of Zhuanxu by raising heaven on the one hand and pushing down on earth on the other, thus cutting off the road to heaven, making mankind clearly understand its limitations and warning it not to indulge in usurpation. From then on Chong became responsible for heaven and Li for earth and gods and men no longer disturbed each other.

Nevertheless, even if Chong and Li had exhausted every possibility, because neither men nor gods could rid themselves of the connection of original essence that joined them, there were still some routes between heaven and earth that remained open. Chong and Li thereupon gathered these as yet unseparated locations together and concentrated them in the great wilderness of the northwest at a place called the Hinge of Heaven where there was a heavenly gate that opened and closed known as Wuju. This was guarded by a square-faced armless god

whose feet protruded from his head. This god was called Wheeze (*Xu*) and breathed in a peculiar way; he breathed out frequently but only drew breath at long intervals. When he exhaled the gods could descend to earth through the gate and, later, when he inhaled, those humans who, through their own efforts, had regained the qualification to enter heaven were able to ascend straight to heaven through the gate.

Zhuanxu, Chong and Li had completed their re-ordering of heaven and earth but the evil in men had not been completely eradicated and still hovered over the world

Mural: *Bu Qianqiu and His Wife Ascending to Immortality* (detail)
Western Han Dynasty
Luoyang
Luoyang Museum of Ancient Art, Henan Province

The Bu Qianqiu Tomb mural was discovered at Luoyang in Henan in 1976 and takes its name from the copper intaglio seal inscribed "seal of Bu Qianqiu" in seal script. The mural is located on the ceiling of the tomb and is formed on the surface of twenty hollow bricks. It shows the imposing spectacle of Bu Qianqiu and his wife ascending in state to the magic realm of Kunlun guided and escorted by Nüwa, Fuxi, Sun, Moon, an alchemical emissary bearing a tablet of office, two dragons, magpies, white tigers and female immortals, all presented in an imaginary world of ordered mystery. The two illustrations are parts of the mural containing a depiction of Fuxi and a toad.

Man Driving a Dragon
Painting on silk
Warring States Period
Height 37.5 cm by width 28 cm
Hunan Provincial Museum

Excavated in 1973 from the Chu period tomb at Danziku in Changsha, Hunan Province. The center of the painting depicts a male wearing a high crown and with a sword at his waist, considered to be the occupant of the tomb. He appears in profile, his hand grasping his sword and standing on the body of a dragon beneath a canopy; the dragon looks up with furled tail, its body in a circle, beside a boat there is an attendant carp. The painting is concise but with a mysterious flavor. Many scholars consider that this is a chart for the ascent to heaven. The image of the man is vividly portrayed, the face is finely delineated and ornament and apparel fluently express the floating quality of the garments. This painting together with *Figure with Dragon and Phoenix* (see page 70) are regarded as the twin pillars of pre-Qin art.

like an epidemic. These roving evil intentions produced some new gods of whom Qiongqi was one. Qiongqi had the form of a ferocious tiger with wings and could fly; he often swooped from the sky and caught up humans to eat. Seeing two humans fighting on earth below, he would devour the one that was honest and principled; hearing of someone who was loyal and trustworthy he would fly down and bite off his nose; learning of somebody who was contumacious and lacking virtue he would catch an animal and present it to him as a gift. With such gods, mankind could no longer rely upon imitation of the gods to regulate their behavior, they had to mobilize their own original essence and re-connect with the Pangu and Nüwa of old and determine right and wrong, truth and error on the basis of their own inner conscience. What inconvenienced mankind the most was that the knowledge and skills formerly bestowed by heaven had been destroyed by the severance of heaven from earth. Mankind would now have to depend upon its own intelligence and wisdom to relearn them.

DWELLING IN NESTS

Ever since the hearts of men had been filled with evil and trickery it had become more difficult for them to live together with beasts and birds. Originally, man had been without cunning, living peaceably amongst the animals and would pull their tails when happy or stroke their beards. But now, as soon as man was moved by thoughts of evil, wild animals and birds of prey, feeling threatened, immediately and swiftly attacked him. To cut a long story short, the animals had seen through mankind's evil intentions and now attacked fiercely without even waiting for man to think evil. In the beginning, infants placed in birds' nests had been thrown out by the birds. Man did not enjoy the possession of teeth and claws, had lost the ability to fly and could not contend with beasts and birds on an equal footing. He could only flee. Sometimes, he fled in such haste that there was no time to take the plant seeds that he had gathered. He gradually seemed unable to carry on. As to a dwelling place, now that he could no longer use birds' nests, he could only suffer the ceaseless onslaughts of nature, endure the damp of dew and frost and the blast of wind and rain.

At this point there appeared a man of remarkable intelligence. He minutely examined the construction of birds' nests and carefully observed the rise and fall of the lay of the land in the hope that he could create a place where man could live. But there was nothing to which he could refer and, intelligent as he was, he spent three years in painful thought without achieving any result. Suddenly, one day, there was a storm of a strength never encountered before and a ferocious wind blew down a great many large trees. Some of these trees fell on top of other trees that had already been blown down, leaving a tiny space beneath. Soaked by the rain and desperate with fear, the shivering people cowered in this tiny space, huddling together for warmth. It so happened that, as he was racking his brains, the man of intelligence observed this scene and there was a faint movement in his mind, as if something had struck it. He knew that he had found a brilliant solution to the problem of a dwelling place for mankind.

After the storm was over, people emerged from their places of refuge to warm themselves in the sun. The man of intelligence called them together on the side of a slope and made them dig out the soil with tree branches and excavate a great cave, high enough for a man to stand and wide enough for people to lie down. When the cave was completed he made them weave the small branches of the fallen trees together into a size that fitted the cave. He then cut a tree into four timbers the height of the cave, set the woven branches at the four corners of the cave to form a roof and used brambles to block the cave entrance. In this way mankind acquired a dwelling that could protect it from wind and rain. The people, who had already had enough of living in the open, were delighted beyond their expectations and stood

gazing at this dwelling in confusion. They did not know what to call it, they just felt that it looked like a bird's nest and so called it a nest (*chao*). The man of intelligence who had taught them how to build this nest dwelling was named a sage with the honorific title of Youchaoshi—the Nesting One.

Because of the existence of dwellings shaped like birds' nests, man later built houses with ridgepoles and rooms; because of the existence of fire, man was later able to make implements and vessels by firing pottery and casting bronze, mankind's knowledge began to develop and civilization took a great step forward. However, all this is for later, and we shall leave it for the moment. There are still many pressing problems waiting for a solution.

Ganlan Type Structure

The present stilt houses of the Tujia people of Hunan are a developed form of the *ganlan* (pole-railing) type structure and their true source may be traced back to the "nest dwellings" of primitive man. A "nest dwelling" is a house built in the branches of a tree and takes its name from its resemblance to a bird's nest. There are a relatively large number of ancient textual references to "nest dwellings" as the origin of the *ganlan* type structure. The *daozhi* chapter of Zhuangzi (late 4th century BC), for example, says: "in ancient times, animals were many but people few, thus people dwelt in nests in order to avoid them." The earliest nest dwellings were in forests, "dwellings of nests in trees" adapted to the life of the hunter-gatherer and a primitive agricultural economy. By the middle of the neolithic period and with the development of an agricultural (plowed) economy, man gradually emerged from the forests and began building houses on slopes or level ground and nest dwellings subsequently developed into the *ganlan* type structure.

THE CREATION OF THE EIGHT TRIGRAMS

After mankind had learned the use of fire and of cultivation, there was still plenty of room left on earth, food and clothing were plentiful, there was no need for these inventions and man could live in ancient tribal settlements that were like a fairyland. One of these settlements was called Huaxuzhou, which lay west of Yanzhou and north of Taizhou. It is not known how many millions of *li* it was in extent. Legend has it that its people were plain and simple in character and were easy-going in the manner of their daily lives. They knew neither the joy of living nor the fear of death; they did not selfishly love themselves nor distance themselves from others and thus were without love or hate and passed the years of their life untroubled. People regarded this place with envy, but it could not be reached by boat, nor by cart and reaching it on foot was unthinkable. All that could be done was to imagine its desirable life in one's dreams.

It is said that in Huaxuzhou there was a great lake called Thunder Lake where the trees grew in dense profusion, the undergrowth was thick and wonderful birds and strange animals came and went. One day, a chaste young maiden went to the lake to play, came across an enormous footprint and, unable to restrain herself, stepped on it. Having taken the step, the maiden felt her heart jolt and her body give an involuntary shudder. She went home and found herself with child. A full thirteen years later she eventually gave birth to a child called Fuxi.

Fuxi had a bulging head and staring eyes, teeth like a turtle and lips like a dragon, eyebrows of white hair and a beard that reached the ground. This child, born in simplicity and pure of character grew slowly to manhood in this fairyland.

Fuxi grew up just at a time when man's material life was becoming richer. In the depths of his heart man sought and aspired after something but, at that time, there was nothing in the realm of man that could give him comfort. However, Fuxi responded to this inner longing; he looked to the heavens for a sign and to the earth for a reason; he observed the form of birds and beasts and took the pulse of the earth; he observed his own body and distant living things, feeling that some silent strength was flowing into his body and that there was something within crying to get out. He was vaguely aware that there was something in the process of creation but could not grasp it. Every day he watched the rushing waters and sensed the unceasing change of the universe, feeling as if there was something immutable within it and that he was about to approach its core.

One day, Fuxi was deep in thought beside a river, his mind as far, far away as the furthest star at the edge of heaven and as deep as the deepest light in the depths of the ocean, murky and indistinct, when he lost the awareness of where he was. Suddenly, a mystic white horse with the head of a dragon leaped from the river, paused for a moment in front of him and then galloped away into

Album: *Ten Thousand Years of the Imperial Succession—Fuxi*

Ming Dynasty
Qiu Ying (c.1501–c.1551)
Ink and color on silk
Height 32.5 cm by width 32.6 cm
Palace Museum, Taibei

The album consists of twenty leaves depicting the images and attainments of well-known Chinese historical figures including Fuxi, Shennong, the Yellow Emperor, Shun, Yu the Great. An inscription in regular script accompanies each image. The album is simply presented and the colors consist mainly of green and green/blue with some gilding. The scenes are fresh and elegant. In the above leaf, Fuxi is seated, the eight trigrams to his right.

the far distance. Fuxi, in his trance, looked blankly at the horse as it emerged from the water and galloped off. In the twinkling of an eye, Fuxi, who had hitherto been pondering the mysteries of heaven and earth, saw clearly the design on the back of the horse and how

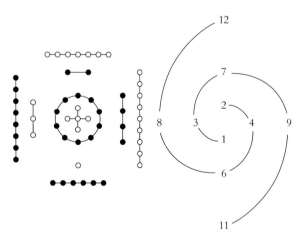

it changed into a circular spiral that spun round and round.

According to tradition the design on the left is the one on the back of the white horse and the one on the right is the spinning spiral that Fuxi saw. Fuxi simplified these black and white spinning shapes into the symbols yin (⚋) and yang (⚊). He then sub-divided these two symbols into eight special symbols, *qian* (☰), *kun* (☷), *zhen* (☳), *xun* (☴), *kan* (☵), *li* (☲), *gen* (☶) and *dui* (☱), that later became known as the eight trigrams. Each trigram had a number of correspondents. For example, *qian* corresponded with heaven, horse, father, and head. *Kun* corresponded with earth, ox, mother and belly. *Zhen* corresponded with thunder, dragon, foot and old male. *Xun* corresponded with wind, chicken, thigh and old woman. *Kan* corresponded with water, pig, ear and middle-aged man. *Li* corresponded with fire, male pheasant, eye, and middle-aged woman. *Gen* corresponded with mountain, dog, hand and young man. *Dui* corresponded with lake, ox, mouth and young woman. The eight trigrams seemed to hold all creation within them, no matter whether of the natural world, the animal world or the world of man and his affairs. Fuxi also refined out the attributes of each symbol, strength from *qian*, obedience from *kun*, action from *zhen*, submission from *xun*, to fall into from *kan*, to adhere from *li*, to cease from *gen*, and to show from *dui*, matching them with the state and laws of the movement of matter. Thereafter, Fuxi made a chart of the eight trigrams arranged in order within a square which included the numerical changes of the river chart, thereby responding to the rise and fall of yin-yang in each symbol.

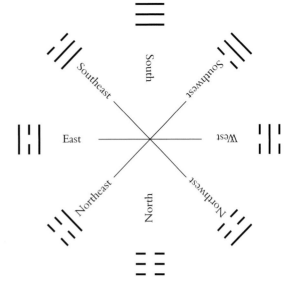

Bronze Eight Trigrams Mirror with Twelve Zodiac Animal Symbols
Southern Song to Yuan Dynasty (1279–1368)
Palace Museum, Taibei

The innermost circle at the center of the mirror consists of the eight trigrams surrounded by an outer circle of the twelve zodiac animals.

This chart is known as the "earlier heaven eight trigram square."

Having thought of the eight trigrams and arranged the earlier heaven eight trigram

square, Fuxi felt as if the words that had been weighing on his heart had been spoken at last. A hitherto unknown and never before imagined world had been opened up and Fuxi seemed to have brought back a treasured hero from the realm of the gods. A summation of all that mankind had previously experienced, including its gradually accumulating knowledge seemed to be contained within these eight infinitely changeable symbols. Most mysterious of all was the fact that because of Fuxi's deep insight into the knowledge he had gained, the eight trigrams were not only a summation of what was already known, they were also a prediction of the future. Of course, this is not to say that it was possible to surmise the inevitabilities of the future on the basis of the eight trigrams and their changes. However, mankind could,

The Zhencheng Building
Yongding County, Longyan City, Fujian Province

Built in 1912 with an area of 5,000 square meters, this building has completely assimilated the idea that "heaven, earth and man are as one" of the *Book of Changes* and was designed and built on the basis of the eight trigrams. The building is divided into inner and outer rings, the outer ring comprising four stories with forty-eight rooms to a story, in a layout of eight trigrams with a superbly effective brick firewall between each trigram. The trigrams are joined by interconnecting doors which when closed form separate independent courtyards. When open the whole building is interlinked into an integral whole.

The *Book of Changes* (*Yijing*)

The book contains Fuxi's description of the eight trigrams, with text by King Wen of Zhou and commentary (*Shi Yi*) by Confucius (511–479 BC). In all, 64 trigrams containing 384 lines. In addition, the *Book of Changes* describes the natural world and records astronomical and climatic changes. It also contains theories of social conduct. It was used by ancient rulers in the implementation of government. It was also used for divination.

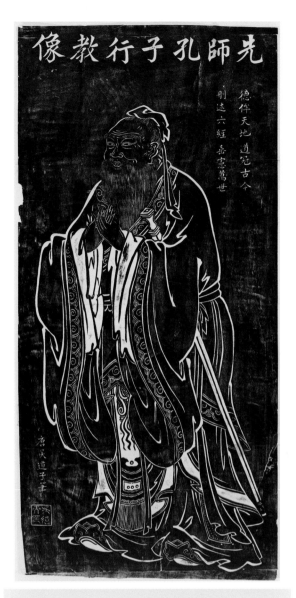

in the future, in moments of inspiration, once more return to Fuxi's concentrated state of mind at the time and see what picture of mankind it contained, and then use that to determine the future, based upon the conditions, good or bad, of its own epoch.

Having produced the eight trigrams, Fuxi then produced a further sixty-four trigrams through a process of doubling. For example, the three lines of *qian* (☰) and *qian* (☰) doubled, produced the six line hexagram *qian* (䷀) ; the three lines of *qian* (☰) and *kun* (☷) doubled, produced the hexagrams *tai* (䷊) and *pi* (䷋). It may be that Fuxi's creation of the eight trigrams was just what mankind anticipated at the time and that in the depths of his heart, man had long hoped for the appearance of a creation such as this. Consequently, with the spread of the eight trigrams and the earlier heaven eight trigram square, mankind felt that it was indeed something that had been a heartfelt hope and longing. Their anxieties eased and their hearts responded sympathetically. Those most deeply affected by this not only quickly mastered the entirety of the eight trigrams and their changes but, following in the footsteps of Fuxi, began their own creative processes.

Stone Rubbing: *The Former Master Confucius Teaching*

Tang Dynasty
Wu Daozi (c. 680–759)
Height 115 cm by width 55 cm
Confucius Museum, Qufu, Shandong Province

Confucius was a famed Chinese thinker, philosopher, educationist and founder of the Confucian school of philosophy. Following its establishment, Confucianism was developed over the years by scholars into an ideological system that became the mainstream of traditional Chinese culture.

This is a Qing Dynasty rubbing of Wu Daozi's stone carving of Confucius. It shows him leaning slightly forward and expresses the "temperate, kind, courteous, restrained and magnanimous" quality of his conduct. With hands clasped and the back of the hands facing outward, a sword at his waist, it shows a sage skilled in matters both civil and military.

Lacquer Box from the Tomb of Marquis Yi of Zeng: the lid displaying the 28 Stellar Mansions

Lacquer Box from the Tomb of Marquis Yi of Zeng

OBSERVING THE HEAVENLY SYMBOLS TO FIX THE CALENDAR

In the past, without clocks or calendar, time, season and position were determined by observation of the sun, moon and stars. Consequently, each star had its own name. Taking the Twenty-Eight Stellar Mansions as an example, the names of the seven mansions of the Blue Dragon of the East are: *jiao* (角), *kang* (亢), *di* (氐), *fang* (房), *xin* (心), *wei* (尾), and *ji* (箕). The seven mansions of the Black Tortoise of the North are: *dou* (斗), *niu* (牛), *nu* (女), *xu* (虚), *wei* (危), *shi* (室), and *bi* (壁). The seven mansions of the White Tiger of the East are *kui* (奎), *lou* (娄), *wei* (胃), *mao* (昴), *bi* (毕),

Lacquer Box from the Tomb of Marquis Yi of Zeng

Warring States Period
Hubei Provincial Museum

A total of five clothes chests were excavated from this tomb at Suizhou in Hubei Province, all containing the clothing of the tomb occupant at the time. The lid of this chest bears an extremely valuable astronomical chart painted in red lacquer. The character "*dou*" symbolizing the Big Dipper is painted on the center of the lid, surrounded by the names of the 28 Stellar Mansions written in seal script. At either end, representing east and west, are the Blue Dragon and White Tiger, two of the four divisions into which the constellations are divided. This is the earliest discovered astronomical material matching all the names of the 28 Stellar Mansions with the Big Dipper and the four divisions, demonstrating that the 28 Stellar Mansions had already been systematized in China at least as early as the early Warring States Period. It also proves that China was one of the earliest countries in the world to have established a system of 28 Stellar Mansions.

zi (觜), and *shen* (参). The seven mansions of the Vermilion Bird of the South are *jing* (井), *gui* (鬼), *liu* (柳), *xing* (星), *zhang* (张), *yi* (翼), and *zhen* (轸). Fuxi created the eight trigrams on the basis of these familiar star names. He now had to try and connect the corresponding trigram symbols and related matter and events on earth to the stars, thus combining the knowledge already acquired into a dynamic whole.

The reason that the seven mansions of the east are named Blue Dragon is because the two stars of the *jiao* mansion resemble the two horns on the head of a dragon; the four stars of the *kang* mansion resemble the dragon's neck, the four stars of the *di* mansion, together with the three stars of the *xin* mansion, resemble the dragon's upper body; the nine stars of the *wei* mansion and the four stars of the *ji* mansion resemble its lower body and the four stars of the *fang* mansion at the center of the seven mansions symbolize the dragon's heart. During winter the seven mansions of the Blue Dragon rise and set with the sun and are invisible to the human eye, almost as if the great dragon formed by this string of stars lies permanently beneath the horizon, so Fuxi named the lowest line of the *qian* (☰) hexagram the "submerged dragon." In the period after the Spring Equinox (*chunfen*), when trees bud and grasses sprout, the seven mansions of the Blue Dragon gradually emerge from the earth's surface and first the head, then the upper half of the body appear above the horizon like a long dragon amidst the fields. So Fuxi described the second

line of the hexagram as "seeing a dragon amongst the fields." After some time, the tail and lower half of the dragon appear above the surface, which looks difficult but changes every day and Fuxi used the simile of the hard working gentleman to describe the third line of the trigram as "laboring all day and vigilant by night," working hard during the day and alert to danger all the time. Finally, the dragon stretches and leaps as its whole body appears above the earth. The description of the trigram's fourth line as "one that leaps from the abyss" exactly resembles a dragon leaping above the horizon.

The Blue Dragon rises gently and moves slowly towards the center of the sky and when people see it hanging almost above their roof tops, a sudden cool breeze and autumn has arrived, precisely the "flying dragon in the sky" of the fifth line in the *qian* hexagram. Thereafter, the seven mansions of the Blue Dragon move gradually from the center of the

On previous spreads
Handscroll: *Gods of the Five Planets and 28 Stellar Mansions*
Southern Dynasty (420–589)
Zhang Sengyou (by transmission) (dates of birth and death unknown)
Ink and color on silk
Height 27.5 cm by length 490 cm
Osaka City Museum of Fine Arts

The ancients believed that every planet and constellation was a god. This handscroll portrays the gods of the five planets and 28 Stellar Mansions. The five planets are Venus (metal), Jupiter (wood), Mercury (water), Mars (fire) and Saturn (earth); originally the 28 Stellar Mansions were the constellations chosen by the ancients as sidereal markers against which to compare the movement of the sun, moon and planets. In this scroll there is one picture to each planet and Stellar Mansions, it may be a female figure, an old man, a youngster, or a figure with the head of an animal on a human body. Only the five planets and 12 Stellar Mansions have survived, suggesting that this scroll is only the first section of the original.

The colored figures in the scroll are delineated in a refined, fluid and delicate way. The oxen, horses and other animals are lively and vivid and the style of the whole is compact and well knit.

sky towards the west and when the dragon's head (*jiao*) and neck (*kang*) gradually sink beneath the western horizon, the weather turns from warm to cold and the Beginning of Winter (*lidong*) has arrived. Thereafter, when the whole body of the Blue Dragon sinks beneath the horizon, hiding there through the endless winter, Fuxi compares this to the "regrets of the over-bearing (*kang*) dragon" of the sixth hexagram line, a play on the meanings of the character *kang*, indicating the need for those in high positions to guard against hubris for fear of subsequent defeat and regret. The process of the Blue Dragon sinking beneath the horizon and the disappearance of the *jiao* mansion constituted by the head and upper body of the dragon followed by the *kang* and *di* mansions so that they became invisible to man was described by Fuxi as "a flight of headless dragons."

It was not just observation of the stars. Later, people copied Fuxi in observing all the changes of the heavens. For example, when they observed the cyclical waxing and waning of the moon they expressed the presence of light by using the yang trigram line (⚊) and the absence of light by using the yin trigram line (⚋). The complete absence of light from the moon on the first day of the lunar month is expressed by the use of the *kun* trigram (☷); the *zhen* trigram (☳) marks the appearance of the pale new moon in the west on the evening of the third day of the lunar month; the eighth day is the increasingly bright first quarter moon in the south represented by the *dui* trigram (☱); the effulgent full moon of the fifteenth day appearing in the east is expressed by the *qian* trigram (☰); on the eighteenth when the moon begins to wane and appears in the west in the early morning with a faint shadow in the lower portion, it is expressed by the *xun* trigram (☴); on the twenty-third, when the third quarter moon appears in the south and the lower portion shadows have increased, it is expressed by the *gen* trigram (☶); finally, on the thirtieth, when there is no light at all from the moon it is once again expressed by the *kun* trigram (☷). The trigrams representing cyclical lunar movement were incorporated with the Ten Heavenly Stems and the trigrams of the earlier heaven square into the diagram below, where the outer anti-clockwise circle contains the Ten Heavenly Stems and the inner clockwise circle is made up of the eight basic trigrams with *qian* (all unbroken yang lines) at the top opposite *kun* (all broken yin lines) at the bottom.

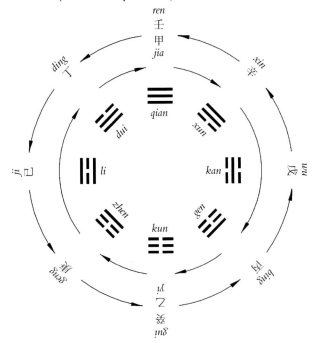

It was further observed that there was a rule governing sunrise and sunset and that the sun only rose from due east and set due west at the Spring Equinox and Autumn Equinox (*qiufen*). The Winter Solstice (*dongzhi*) marks the day of the sun's most southerly declination and the Summer Solstice (*xiazhi*), the day of its most northerly declination. Consequently the *kun* hexagram (☷) was used to express the shortest day of the year at the Winter Solstice and the *qian* hexagram (☰) to express the longest day at the Summer Solstice. The Spring Equinox was expressed by the *tai* hexagram (䷊) and the Autumn Equinox by the *pi* hexagram (䷋).

From the day of the Winter Solstice, the days begin to lengthen and it was regarded as the return of the yang principle and was expressed by the use of the *fu* hexagram (䷗). When the various significances of these individual symbols are further incorporated with the Ten Heavenly Stems and Twelve Earthly Branches, together with the earlier trigram square, the result is the diagram below, where the outermost circle of hexagrams proceeds anti-clockwise from the all yang *qian* hexagram, through the all yin *kun* hexagram and round to *qian* again, losing and gaining yang and yin elements on the way. The inner circle contains the original eight trigrams aligned with the points of the compass, south at the top, north at the bottom. The outer circle is aligned with the Stems and Branches.

On the basis of these astronomical changes, Fuxi determined spring, summer, autumn and winter and combined them with the trigram symbols. Following very many years of laborious searching in the manner of Fuxi, the two solstices and the two equinoxes were incorporated with the Ten Heavenly Stems, the Twelve Earthly Branches and the five elements and their relative affinities

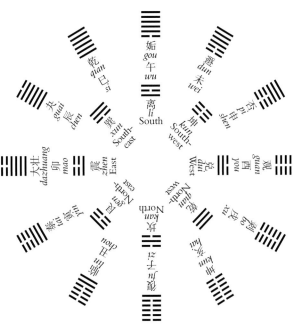

Mural: *Four Spirits in the Cloud*

Length 5.1 m by width 3.27 m
Early Western Han Dynasty
Henan Museum

Excavated in 1987 from the Persimmon Orchard Tomb of the King of Liang Tomb Complex at Mangdangshan in Yongcheng, Henan Province. The mural is on the ceiling of the tomb and displays, at its center, an enormous seven meter long flying dragon with a Vermilion Bird to the east and a White Tiger to the west, all surrounded by mythical animals and a pattern of *lingzhi* fungus and cloud. The mural starts at the western extremity of the ceiling of the main tomb and extends eastwards for more than three meters with an overall area of 30 square meters. It fills the gaps in the history of Western Han wall paintings and is some 600 years earlier than the murals at Dunhuang. Not only is it earlier, more completely preserved and extensive in area than anything seen before in China, but it also sustains within it the epic magnificence of China's early Han belief in immortality and the supernatural. Its art historical value is extremely high.

(*wuxing shengke*) into symbols representing all kinds of time, position, and direction. These verified time symbols, derived from man's knowledge of the world, became the calendar system. Later, man thought up a practical means of using this theoretical knowledge for the purpose of better instruction and circulation, but that is another story.

The Twenty-Four Solar Terms

An ancient Chinese division of the year into seasons based upon the operation of annual climatic phenomena. The terms are: Beginning of Spring (*lichun*), Rain Water (*yushui*), Insect Wake (*jingzhe*), Spring Equinox (*chunfen*), Pure Brightness (*qingming*), Grain Rain (*guyu*), Start of Summer (*lixia*), Lesser Full Grain (*xiaoman*), Grain in Beard (*mangzhong*), Summer Solstice (*xiazhi*) , Lesser Heat (*xiaoshu*), Greater Heat (*dashu*), Beginning of Autumn (*liqiu*), End of Heat (*chushu*), White Dew (*bailu*), Autumn Equinox (*qiufen*), Cold Dew (*hanlu*), Frost Descends (*shuangjiang*), Beginning of Winter (*lidong*), Lesser Snow (*xiaoxue*), Greater Snow (*daxue*), Winter Solstice (*dongzhi*), Lesser Cold (*xiaohan*), and Great Cold (*dahan*).

The Twenty-Four Solar Terms were established prior to the Qin Dynasty (221–206 BC) and were codified in the Han Dynasty as a supplementary calendar for the regulation of agriculture. They are a knowledge system of annual seasons, climate and natural phenomena based upon observation of the movement of the sun throughout the solar year. They divide the sun's annual course into twenty-four sections, each section constituting a solar term, starting with the Beginning of Spring and ending with the Great Cold and then completing the cycle by returning to the beginning. They were issued by government offices throughout successive dynasties as a yardstick for measuring time and were also a compass for the direction of agricultural production and for forecasting hot and cold and snow and rain in everyday life. They were a crystallization of the long accumulated experience and wisdom of the Chinese working people.

The Twenty-Four Solar Terms were formally recorded by UNESCO as part of Mankind's Intangible Cultural Heritage on 30th November 2016.

AUSPICIOUS DRAGON AND PHOENIX

Man cannot run fast and so his feet gave birth to wheels; his hands are weak and feeble and his strength thus unlimited; he cannot fly and so there are wings; he cannot swim and so can dive deep into the ocean; his teeth are not sharp and so has grown fangs; he cannot see far and so we have the God of the All Seeing Eye; he cannot hear everything and so we have the God of the All Hearing Ear ... he never blunders because there is no existence to reality, only our imagination can produce something from nothing and realize the wonders around us.

Following the felling of Jianmu and the separation of heaven and earth, man could

Figure with Dragon and Phoenix
Painting on silk
Warring States Period
Height 31 cm by width 22.5 cm
Hunan Provincial Museum

Excavated in 1949 from the Chu Tomb at Chenjiadashan in Changsha, this painting on silk is simple in composition but profound in artistic concept. It is also one of the earliest surviving and most complete portraits discovered in China. The painting is divided into upper, middle, and lower levels. The upper level consists of a dragon and a phoenix, the phoenix with neck stretched, head lifted and wings raised upwards; two horns grow from the dragon's head and its body is twisted as if in full flight; the middle level is a lady of the nobility in profile and is an image of the occupant of the tomb; the lower level represents what appears to be a receptacle in the shape of a bent moon which may be a boat made from a single tree trunk carrying the soul to heaven. There is considerable expressive power in the stark contrast between the sense of movement in the depiction of the dragon and the phoenix and the still repose of the lady.

no longer climb up to the heavens. But we should remember that although Nüwa made man from earth and although the material she used was mud from the riverbank, she had also breathed on man and this breath was the original essence that gave birth to Pangu. This breath of original essence, that co-existed with heaven and earth, encouraged man ever upwards in an urge to understand more and more of the secrets of heaven and earth. Men hoped for some device that would, once more, connect them with heaven. It was like this: it was impossible that man, crowned and caped with cloud, could soar to a height of over a thousand *li*, so, as a result, there appeared the multi-colored phoenix; it was impossible for man to upset rivers and overturn the ocean or ride the clouds, so, as a result, dragons appeared.

See, where the sun rises, a multi-colored bird hovers with trembling wings, its whole body bathed in the pink light of dawn, glowing in brilliant colors. This is the phoenix; it perches at an outpost close to the sun, cawing at the dawn. The birds under the heavens hear and fly towards it, almost obscuring the sun's rays. Sometimes the phoenix performs a solitary dance, as fickle in form as the wind itself. Usually it stays hidden away but when it appears all is peace. It is the Black Swallow, the Vermilion Bird, the fabulous Peng Bird, its back like the clouds that hang from heaven, that, when storms arise, flies three thousand *li* over the sea towards the Pool of Heaven, its wings striking the waves and then

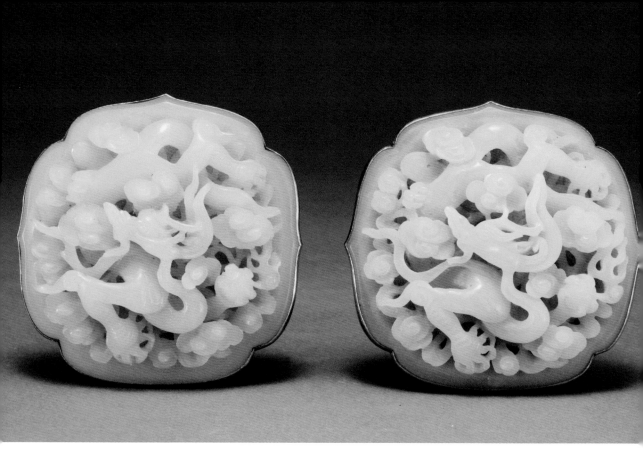

rises in a whirlwind for ninety thousand *li*.

It seems to have chosen the advantages of all the animals of the world to make up its body. In front, a wild goose, behind, a unicorn. It has the neck of a snake and the tail of a fish, the forehead of a stork and as many feathers as a mandarin duck. It has the chin of a swallow and the mouth of a cockerel but eyes like a man and ears like an owl. It has the legs of a crane and the talons of an eagle. Its back bears a dragon pattern, its body is the shape of a tortoise and its tail curls away forever and displays like a peacock. This splendid multi-colored phoenix often glides above the luxuriant paulownia trees, and then a full five hundred years later collects scented wood and first immolates and, then, resurrects itself. From thereon, strange and beautiful, it is immortal.

See, suddenly from the silent depths, a great fish leaps and the white waves billow to the edge of heaven. In the twinkling of an eye, the fish changes shape and whirls dancing in the sky, the weather grows angry and waves appear on the calm blue sea. This great Blue Dragon, which swims in water, flies in the air and walks on land. It summons the wind and calls the rain, races the clouds and rides the mist. It is both bright and yet dark, short and yet long. In spring it ascends the heavens and

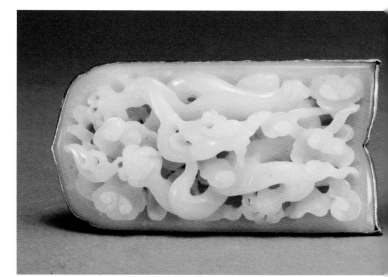

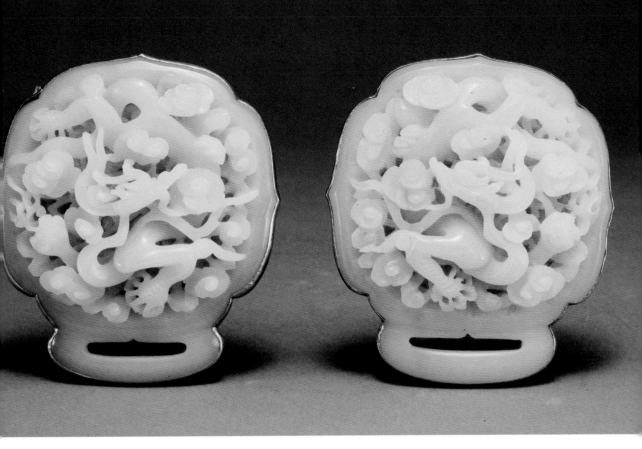

in autumn returns to the abyss. Its head is visible but not the tail, its comings and goings are invisible to mere mortals but it drives a dragon chariot through the high heavens.

It is like thunder and lightning, cloud and mist, rainbow and shadow, ever changing, mysterious and unfathomable in its coming and going. It has the head of a horse, the nose of an elephant, the horns of a deer, the mane

Gold Inlaid Jade Belt Plaques with a Dragon and Cloud Pattern (part)

Ming Dynasty
Sunflower Shaped Ornament: overall length 8.8 cm by width 7.9 cm
Side Plaques: overall length 8.4 cm by width 4.2 cm
Nanjing Municipal Museum

Excavated from the Tomb of Wang Xingzu, erected in the 4th year of the Ming Emperor Hongwu (1368–1398). The tomb is located at Zhangjiawa in the Drum Tower District of Nanjing. The belt is made up of 14 jade plaques carved from pure smooth white Hetian jade on an inlaid gold base. The carving of the main plaques is reticulated in several layers that display the upper and lower coils of a dragon's body. The dragon's head is finely carved with beard, whiskers, eyebrows and mane as well as horns, nose, lips and jaw, in an accurate representation of the awe-inspiring aspects of a dragon. The dragon itself is surrounded by a pattern containing the *lingzhi* fungus and clouds, just as if it were really bursting through a layer of clouds. Each plaque is finely and exquisitely carved, well able to bear a reputation as a masterpiece of the art of jade carving in ancient China.

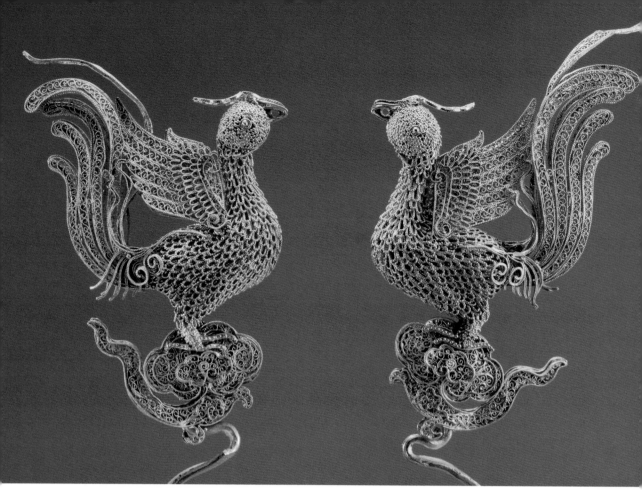

Gold Hairpins in the Form of a Phoenix (detail)

Ming Dynasty
Overall length 22.3 cm by width 6.3 cm
Nanjing Municipal Museum

Excavated from the Tomb of Zhu, the wife of Xu Fu, erected in the 12th year of the Ming Emperor Zhengde (1506–1521). The tomb is located at Bancangcun in the Xuanwu District of Nanjing. Made of lustrous gold, one piece measures 22.3 cm and the other 22 cm. The pins are flat and their tips, unlike the generality of pins, are bent into the shape of a hook. The upper ends are also bent where they join the head of the pin. The head of the pin has been modeled into the shape of a phoenix dancing in the sky. It has a pointed beak, broad wings, up-turned phoenix eyes, and stands with head raised and breast extended. The wings, with layer upon layer of slightly raised feathers, are spread as if about to fly and the bird stands upon clouds shaped like a *ruyi* scepter. Whilst pursuing the concept of representative form, the whole model also emphasizes the nobility of the phoenix, symbolizing grandeur and good fortune. It is a valuable and exquisite work of art.

of a stallion, the body of a snake, the scale of a fish, the fangs of a crocodile, the tail of a fish, the talons of an eagle, the feet of an alligator, the belly of a sea-serpent, the eyes of a rabbit, the ears of an ox and the paws of a tiger. There are eighty-one scales on its back, whiskers round its mouth, a jewel beneath its chin and reversed scales at its throat. The horns on its head are like a Boshan Burner and with them it enters and leaves heaven and earth, bringing the news of heaven to mankind. Its breath becomes cloud, it is skilled at creating water, it can breathe fire and as it moves cloud and waters rage, when it is still the skies are clear and the sun bright. It never travels with a companion but flies alone between heaven and earth, its scales and talons now visible and then invisible.

Dragon and phoenix appeared, man retrofitted them with legends and, through inversion, these latecomers somehow became the ancestors of all living things— phoenix gave birth to the mystic bird Luan and Luan begat ordinary birds, the ancestor birds of all feathered things; the dragon Ying—the flying dragon, begat Jianma and

Dragon (*Long*)

A mysterious legendary animal with a long snake-like body, scales and claws. It can raise clouds and cause rain, chief of all watery beasts.

Phoenix (*Fenghuang*)

According to ancient legend, the king of the birds. The male is known as a *feng* and the female as a *huang*. The composite name is *fenghuang*. The feathers are of five colors and its call resembles the music of panpipes. Often used to represent an auspicious omen.

Auspicious Dragon and Phoenix

Usually refers to propitious or festive matters or events. In Chinese tradition dragon and phoenix represent good fortune and heart's desire. Used together they more often indicate festive jubilation. A colored glaze, narrow necked vase excavated from the Beishouling Yangshao Culture site at Baoji in Shaanxi Province bears a dragon phoenix pattern. This cultural treasure demonstrates that the origins of both dragon and phoenix lie in the New Stone Age of seven to eight thousand years ago, and that the two are synchronous.

Born of the distant past and bearers of rich cultural phenomena, the dragon and phoenix are the seal, insignia, symbol and emblem of the Chinese race. The dragon possesses the magical characteristics of enjoying water, love of flying, familiarity with the heavens, mutability, mystery, presaging the auspicious, foretelling disaster and displaying power. The phoenix enjoys the magical characteristics of love of fire, association with the sun, the maintenance of virtue, foretelling the auspicious, majesty, valuing purity, displaying beauty and as a metaphor for passion. The complementary and corresponding elements of these magical characteristics drew the dragon and phoenix together, one the ruler of beasts, the other lord of birds; one mutable, soaring, mysterious, the other elegant, virtuous and auspicious. This relationship of collaborative virtue between the two established, in the end, the concept of the "Auspicious Dragon and Phoenix."

Dish with Dragon and Phoenix

Ming Dynasty
Porcelain painted with cobalt blue under and colored enamels over transparent glaze (Jingdezhen ware)
Height 7 cm, diameter 37.5 cm, diameter of rim 37.8 cm, diameter of foot 24.4 cm
Metropolitan Museum of Art, New York

During the period of Shenzong (1573–1620), the Ming Emperor Wanli, there was an official handicrafts fashion for the production of brightly colored objects, principally as metaphors of good fortune. It included a multitude of eye-catching subjects designed to create a rich, vibrant atmosphere. This five-colored dragon and phoenix patterned dish is painted with a five-clawed dragon and a phoenix. The dragon represents the emperor and the phoenix usually represents the empress.

Dragon Pattern Luohan *Shuyao* Couch-Bed

Qing Dynasty
Palace Museum, Taibei

This red sandalwood dragon pattern Luohan (Arhat) couch-bed is in the three-sided screen style. The couch surround is densely carved with a pattern of two dragons facing each other as they pierce the clouds, five claws outstretched towards the flaming pearl in the center. The back section of the surround shows five bats (*fu*) hovering loosely in a cloud, each bat in a different pose with the meaning of "the arrival of the five blessings (*fu*)."

The use of sandalwood in the construction of a Luohan couch-bed is extremely rare and confined to the imperial family.

Jianma begat the Qilin, the ancestor of ordinary beasts, the ancestor beasts of all furred things; the dragon Jiao begat Kungeng who begat Jianxie who begat ordinary fish, the ancestor fish of all things with scales; the dragon Xian begat the turtle Xuanyuan who begat the Linggui turtle who begat ordinary turtles, the ancestor turtles of all things with shells. Once possessed of the mystical dragon and phoenix, man then wove all the later countless auspicious omens, disparate legends, strange animals, fascinating people and spirits, even man's knowledge of the calendar and climate, into legends that were related to them.

Nowadays, man relies on these two beings, dragon and phoenix, to take him on journeys of the imagination to the heights of heaven, the depths of the ocean and to all the vastness of the earth. Now, with the aid of dragon and phoenix, mankind can stealthily evade the solemn command that separated earth from heaven and rush headlong wherever it wishes. It can transcend the bounds of time and space and visit Fuxi, the creator of the eight trigrams, Shennong, who taught mankind about planting and sowing and Suirenshi who drilled fire from wood; man can visit the sacred Kunlun Mountain to see the road to heaven and go to the borders of the northwest and see the rock that Nüwa used to repair the vault of heaven and visit the river bank where she created man, and that first beginning where Pangu opened up earth and heaven. Man can see Cang Jie, the inventor of the written character, Yu the Great who controlled the floods, and the dispositions at the legendary battle of Zhuolu; he can see how images of dragon and phoenix carved on stone continuously changed throughout different eras. Finally, under a colored canopy of auspicious cloud, dragon and phoenix gradually come together in a dance to form a flag that flies in our imagination, symbolizing the peoples raised on earth.

Dragon Crowned Phoenix Ornamental Jade

Late Shang Dynasty
Length 11.3 cm, width 5 cm, thickness 0.3 cm
Palace Museum, Taibei

This jade ornament is formed from a combination of dragon and phoenix and is of a characteristically Shang design. The head of the phoenix bears an S-shaped dragon with an arched back and curled tail.

SHENNONG THE FLAME EMPEROR

Once she had completed the creation of man, Nüwa was exhausted in body and spirit. She rested awhile in the hill forests bordered by the Ji and Jiang rivers and gazed down on her progeny as they thrived and multiplied below. In their multitudes they foraged for food, sought warmth and shelter from the cold, pursued and fought, played together, escaped from wild beasts, found water and lodging and dwelt safely by the hills. Ever since they had taken their first steps on earth, they had cautiously crossed rivers, climbed mountain peaks and looked out on the world. They had emerged from the forests into the open spaces, felt the warmth of the sun and the sound of the water and the damp chill of ice and snow. The days lengthened and time passed, their limbs flexed and their minds grew quick.

Amongst Nüwa's progeny was a clever, healthy girl of the Youjiaoshi clan called Fubao. One bright sunny day, when the tribe was out gathering wild fruit and had reached a lush meadow, she plucked flowers and made them into a garland which she placed on her head as she went further and further into the undergrowth to catch the colored butterflies that appeared one moment and disappeared

Shennong and Fuxi
Qing Dynasty
Anonymous
Ink and color on silk
Height 125.4 cm by width 88.2 cm
Freer and Sackler Galleries, Washington D. C.

the next. Suddenly, unbeknownst to her, the weather closed in, dense black clouds gathered, a border of flame pierced the cloud and struck the enormous tree in front of her, there was a flash and a dragon embraced the terrified Fubao, a sudden roll of thunder and heaven and earth spun around her. When the remainder of the tribe caught up with her, the wind had dropped and the thunder ceased, all had returned to normal.

Thereafter, Fubao became pregnant and bore a son on the banks of the Jiang River, a child with a human face but the countenance of a dragon, one that could command all living things. Just as Fubao delivered her child, a spring with nine eyes or openings suddenly appeared, each eye was connected with the others, so that taking water from one eye caused waves to appear in the eight others. The tribes people believed that there must be some divine purpose to this and cherished and guarded Fubao's son, quietly waiting for him to grow to manhood. Because they lived on the banks of the Jiang River, he was honored with the name Jiang. Later, one day when she was on the banks of the Ji River, Fubao saw the Big Dipper surrounded by lightning that lit up the wastes around her, the light flashed through her body and in response she became pregnant with a child called Ji.

The two children grew up in different places and when they were adults, each secured the allegiance of the peoples round them, formed into groups, worked together, chose leaders, produced sons and heirs and marked out new territory, improved living conditions and established two neighboring fraternal tribes in the area of Qishan in the Guanzhong plain in Shaanxi, the Jiangshi and Jishi, both brothers holding half the world each. These became Shennong the Flame Emperor and Yellow Emperor of later generations. The two tribes inter-married and exchanged their products but because of the rapid growth of their populations there was a shortage of food and adjacent groups raided each other for crops and cattle. The Flame Emperor was skilled in the use of fire and the Yellow Emperor in the use of water but the Yellow Emperor's clan held the upper hand. Chiyou was unprincipled and attacked the vassal kings remorselessly driving out the Flame Emperor. However, a number of wise men in the following of Chiyou became disillusioned with his violence and usurpation and at the great battle of Zhuolu fought against him on the side of the Yellow Emperor and the Flame Emperor. Chiyou was heavily defeated. The Yellow Emperor called on the vassal kings at the battle of Zhuolu and secured their support. He became master of the central plain and established his capital first at Zhuolu, the site of the battle (present-day Hebei) and then at Xinzheng (present-day Henan) and Shouqiu (present-day Shandong).

Rivers of blood flowed at the battle of Zhuolu, the land was laid waste and homes reduced to ruin. The Flame Emperor led the remnants of his clan south east and moved to the south leaving the battle far behind. One day, the Flame Emperor at the head of a number of his followers set out to inspect the living conditions of his clan. In the bitter wind, he saw thinly clad clan members, young and old, faces pinched with cold, searching for grass seed hidden by the snow and crying out with joy at the discovery of the least bit of food. On another hillside he saw a group of people squaring up for a fight over a dead deer, he rushed forward, established the cause and at his bidding both sides shook hands in harmony. The Flame Emperor continued on and met a mother carrying her starving child and wailing in grief, she made the tearful accusation that her family was dying of starvation one by one because of lack of food.

The Flame Emperor mulled over these matters night and day, for the people to eat grass and drink water, pluck fruit from the trees and collect shellfish to assuage their hunger was no plan for the long term. He called a meeting of the leaders of each clan to discuss how to solve the problem of food. Some said that their tribe had lost people to starvation too; others that in their tribe the grass seed kept for winter was eaten as soon as people saw it; some said that the kill from hunting in winter could not compare with that of spring and summer. The discussion went back and forth, how could the system of relying on heaven for food be improved? One elder asked whether they could collect some seed and plant it by the river? The Flame Emperor felt that this was sensible, concentrating sowing and growing together would be convenient for picking. Another clever old hunter asked whether it possible to corral and domesticate the wild animals they had caught and use their offspring for supply during the winter when it was not possible to hunt. Docile animals could also be of help. Finally, the Flame Emperor and the tribal leaders decided that they should plant and grow grain themselves and should also domesticate wild animals.

In a search for the best seed grain, the Flame Emperor led his people across rivers and over hills, through mountains and across ridges. As they went, so they searched, and when they found, they compared what they found with what they had, keeping only the lustrous, many-eared heads of grain and rejecting the withered and diseased. Nevertheless, their harvest was meagre. So they marched for seven days and seven nights and when they were exhausted in body and spirit, a phoenix, its body like an iridescent cloud, appeared flying from the direction of the sun. Dazzled by the gorgeous sight, they stood rooted to the spot gazing at it. In its beak it carried a grass of nine heads and as it flew above them a fine rain of glistening golden grain fell to earth at a sunlit spot not far away. The Flame Emperor led his people in a rush to this spot, finding, when they arrived, not the grain shining with a golden light but a field of tender green shoots sprouting from the earth. The tips of these seedlings were much longer than normal and the grain rounder and fuller. Seeing such a fine crop, the emperor and his people were speechless with excitement. Finally, no longer must they watch their families die through lack of food or their clan fighting amongst each other.

Apart from securing good strains of grain, the Flame Emperor set about teaching his people how to sow the five cereals and surveyed the aridity, rainfall, fertility and height of the land for the sowing of different kinds of cereals. He also invented such aids to agriculture as the plow and the taming of oxen to pull it, and the rearing of dogs, pigs, and horses. He also invented the process of soaking seed in horse urine as a protection against insect damage; he further divided the sowing of different cereals according to the fertility of the soil and achieved a sensible use of differing soils.

During the era of Shennong, people usually gathered wild fruit, consumed cereals, and ate meat and shellfish. They also had to withstand the seasonal changes of weather, to labor and to hunt and to move from place to place, frequently encountering injury and illness. If they fell ill or caught the plague they faced death. Where sickness spread, flourishing villages fell into ruin and bustling villages changed to desolation. Shennong was filled with great compassion for the people. Sickness was a plight that wrenched at his heart.

Stone Relief Rubbing: *Shennong*
Late Eastern Han Dynasty
Wuliang Family Ancestral Hall, Jiaxiang County, Shandong Province

In this stone relief rubbing, Shennong is depicted holding a kind of plow (*lei*) the front part of which is divided into two prongs. The *lei* is one of the earliest plow-type tools known in China. According to legend, the *lei* was invented by Shennong. The *Book of Changes*, compiled in the Warring States Period records that: "After the death of Fuxi, Shennong arose. He carved wood to make a plowshare (*si*) and bent wood to form a *lei*. They were convenient for tilling the soil and clearing undergrowth and he taught all the people of the earth." There is an explanatory inscription alongside the image of Shennong in the Wuliang Ancestral Hall, the general sense of which is that Shennong, on the basis of appropriate natural conditions, taught the populace how to undertake agricultural production and to till the soil and plant cereals, thereby coming to the aid of the wider population.

One day, at dusk, Shennong and his followers were approaching a hamlet in the land of Chu when, at a distance of several *li*, he smelt a dreadful odor. In order to discover its source, he went straight to the center of the village where he found a dozen or more stretchers woven from tree boughs placed in a circle with five or six survivors at their last gasp kneeling beside the stretchers pleading with heaven to rid them of this disaster. A shaman, dressed as the exorcist spirit Fangxiang, the palms of his hands covered in bearskin, the upper part of his body dressed in red and the lower half in black, sharp arrows hanging from his waist and with a shield in his left hand and an axe in his right was dancing and chanting. He then drew a bow of peach wood, fitted arrows of thorn and loosed them towards the four points of the compass, all the while cursing that most evil of all devils, Boqiang.

"Boqiang! Boqiang! See my bow! See my arrows! Go hide amidst the waves of the Eastern Ocean!"

"Go hide in the dense forests of the east!"

"Go hide in the waste lands of the west!"

"Go hide in the dark caves of the south!"

The shaman repeated this three times, the dust rose around him as, soaked in sweat, he was gripped by a convulsion, bow and arrow fell to the ground and his body gradually withered and shrank. Shennong hurried forward to support him and the dying shaman, his expression dimming, told him: "Magic cannot rid us of this plague, the terrible task of saving the suffering people from sickness must pass to you."

In grief, Shennong closed the eyes of the shaman and said to the people: "The shaman has been struck down by the plague, the power of spirits cannot solve this, we must rely on ourselves, we must find a way to rid ourselves of the suffering of sickness." Shennong made suitable arrangements for the handling of the affairs of the clan and pondered the problem

of getting rid of sickness time and again. It so happened that the Country of the White People had just presented a two-thousand-year-old immortal animal called Chenghuang as tribute. It resembled a fox with horns and knew healing and medicine. The Country of the White People lay north of the dwelling of the Dragon Fish and south of the country of the Sushen. The White People were a tribe of the northwest, white in body and with disheveled hair. When they were ill they patted the medicinal animal and spoke a few words to it in their language and the animal went into the wild and returned with a stem of grass in its mouth. They pulped the grass into a juice and when the sick person drank it they recovered immediately. Later, the Yellow Emperor ordered his minister, Fenghou, to note down which plant was effective against which sickness and to take medicine accordingly; most were effective. On this basis, Shennong set out determined to lead his adherents to the four corners of the earth to find and identify every plant, to make medicine and to make a detailed record of it for the treatment of sickness amongst the people.

At the head of Chenghuang and his followers Shennong led the search for medicinal herbs. The earth was vast, the

mountains high and the waters distant. Different plants grew in different places and some plants even grew at the top of cliffs and precipices where the footprint of man was rarely seen. Shennong and his party moved forward along a route that followed the mountain ridges, climbing cliffs, crossing ravines and ditches, flooded rivers and mountain gorges, covering almost every mountain and known river. Sometimes, he would taste seventy different kinds of plant in a day.

As night approached, when the dark blue of the sky appeared even more lonely and remote in contrast with the earth and the sound of birds and animals floated off and on from the distance, Shennong and his followers sat on the hillside and lit a fire, recalling each medicinal plant that they had tasted that day. They carefully noted down the mountain, place and general position of the plant, its shape and color, and even which part of it was effective as a medicine and what illnesses it could treat.

Shennong and his companions also had to check the poison in medicinal plants and how best to use them. Very poisonous plants had to be identified to avoid them being eaten by mistake. Shennong took all upon his own shoulders and some poisonous plants caused

Stone Relief: *Shennong Tasting Herbs*
Eastern Han Dynasty
Sichuan Museum

Excavated at Baozishan, Xinjin County, Sichuan Province in 1951. Stone boxes bearing a carved image are funerary items frequently encountered in Han Dynasty Sichuan and were used both in cave tombs and stone structure tombs. Stone boxes are also known as cliff coffins, carved directly from the cliff wall and immovable. Their images combine the arts of painting and carving, giving a strong impression of visual beauty and providing a vivid picture of Han life and the Han concepts of the universe and of life and death. In this representation (in the middle), Shennong is seen with a staff in one hand and tasting herbs with the other.

great damage to his body. Fortunately, there was a tea-like plant called *tu* that could help relieve the poison but it was relief only, it did not entirely dispel the poison buried deep within his body and his health became worse and worse.

On the slopes of a mountain in Yanling, Shennong discovered a strange, hitherto unknown, plant. It had small yellow flowers, rather like the *tu* plant. One young man shouted jubilantly: "A *tu* plant! A *tu* plant! We can give it to Shennong to cure the poison!" He put out his hand to take the plant when the leaves rustled and curled up like a caterpillar and they all stepped back. Shouting: "Don't move!" Shennong stopped

Chinese Medicine

Based on the theories of traditional Chinese medical science, it fully reflects the characteristics of the natural resources, history and culture of China. It is an ancient Chinese way of healthcare and healing which played a major role in the survival of man in ancient society.

Through observation and experimentation, primitive man came to recognize the host of germs around him and to the greatest extent possible used the roots, stem leaves and fruit of plants together with the viscera, skin, bones and internal organs of animals and some minerals as medicine. Since plants constitute the major part of Chinese medicine, it is also known as Chinese herbal medicine, and in works on Chinese medicine it is referred to as *"ben cao"* (*materia medica*). The earliest known example is the *Materia Medica of Shennong* (*Shennong Bencao Jing*), the author is not known but based on the place names it records it may be a revision of a previous author's work made by a physician of the Eastern Han Dynasty.

On facing page
Moxibustion (detail)

Southern Song Dynasty
Li Tang (1066–1150)
Ink and color on silk
Height 68.8 cm by width 58.7 cm
Palace Museum, Taibei

This is a transmitted copy of a work by the well-known painter Li Tang depicting a scene of medical treatment in an ancient village. In the shade of a roadside tree, a village doctor is administering moxibustion treatment to a patient. Back bent and with moxibustion stick in hand, he strains single-mindedly to apply it with care to the sufferer's back. The patient, with an expression of pain, sits on the ground with his emaciated upper body exposed. His hands and feet are grasped by others to prevent movement and bystanders look on with sympathetic expressions. A boy stands behind the doctor holding a paste plaster ready to apply to the patient's back.

This painting expresses its artistry with delicacy. The figures are depicted with fine brushwork, facial expressions are richly portrayed and there is not a hair out of place. The modeling is both accurate and vivid and the whole is a realistic reflection of popular customs of the time.

Copper Model Demonstrating Acupuncture Points

Ming Dynasty
Hubei Provincial Museum

This is a model of a boy from ancient times, height 86.5 cm. The expression is serene. As many as several hundred acupuncture points cover the whole body. The boy stands with one leg straightened and one bent, one hand is held up and the other hangs loosely. This pose tends to expose the position of all the body's acupuncture points and makes it easier for the practitioner to become familiar with them. It is apparent that whoever cast this copper model expended much thought on its design.

The Classic of Tea (Cha Jing)

In the history of the development of Chinese culture, everything that has to do with the origins of agriculture or plants has always been attributed to Shennong. In his work *The Classic of Tea*, the Chinese God of Tea, Lu Yu (733–804), says: "Tea as a drink began with Shennong." *The Classic of Tea* is the earliest existing, most complete, and most comprehensive specialist introduction to tea in China and even the world. It has become famous as the "Encyclopedia of Tea" and is a comprehensive treatise that covers the history of tea production, its origins and present situation, production techniques, the art of tea drinking and the principles of the Way of Tea. Not only is it a groundbreaking work of agricultural science, it is also a description of the culture of tea. It elevates the ordinary business of tea into a wonderful cultural skill and has promoted the development of Chinese tea culture.

the young man and gingerly plucked a leaf. The moment it was in his mouth, his gut split in pieces and blood gushed from his nose and mouth, there was no time to take tea as an antidote and Shennong died of poisoning.

All were broken-hearted at his parting; they crowned him with a garland of the five cereals and prepared him a bed of thousands of budding medicinal plants. The line of mourners extended for dozens of *li* covering hill and dale. In order to commemorate his benevolence and achievements he was made the God of Medicine and a temple was erected in his name with sacrifices at the four seasons and a Shennong mound was built with a luxuriant grove of medicinal plants in front of it.

Our forefathers achieved a peaceful and stable life. Once, in the depths of night when the noise of man was stilled and the moon hung in the sky, a shooting star streaked across the heavens and a child shouted with surprise. His father said: "That is the soul of one of the departed." The child asked his father: "Where do we go when we die?" "We go home," the father replied. The child asked: "Then where do we come from?" The father fell deep in thought. The world was so vast and man so insignificant. Who was he? He came from far distant Qishan in Guanzhong, he had led his clan east and south, he had stood guard over them, he had cooked food and found warmth, he had grown cereals and vegetables, he was "Shennong the Flame Emperor, God of Agriculture," he had cleared all before him, he had rushed in pursuit, he was the reincarnation of all who had sought the recurring images of the multitudinous history of their ancestors.

Lu Yu Making Tea (detail)

Yuan Dynasty
Zhao Yuan (dates of birth and death unknown)
Ink on paper
Height 27 cm by width 78 cm
Palace Museum, Taibei

Lu Yu, the author of the *Classic of Tea*, was a life-long addict of tea devoted to the Way of Tea and skilled in its appreciation through tasting. In this painting, hills rise and fall in the middle distance and a thatched pavilion has been erected by the stream where trees shelter it from the sun. Lu Yu is seated on the matting whilst, at the side, a boy servant prepares tea. There is an inscription in the artist's hand: "Lu Yu Making Tea." The painting expresses the hermit like leisure and the aspiration towards simplicity of a gentleman of culture.

Zhao Yuan was a late Yuan Dynasty painter skilled in Chinese landscape painting who followed Dong Yuan (?–c. 962) in style and Wang Meng (1308–1385) in technique. He excelled in the use of thick ink on a dry brush.

DRILLING WOOD FOR FIRE

In the south, there is a country called Suiming, beyond the light of sun and moon, where night and day are the same and the seasons never change. There is no end to the darkness of night and people live forever, groping about and calling out to each other amidst the chaos. Sons and heirs are born, and children seem to stop when they are fully grown. Day succeeds day and year follows year and if they cannot bear this desolate lonely existence, they climb to heaven to find another country. In this country, there grows a kind of fire tree, thick and tall, thrusting through the clouds, twisting and turning, obscuring all around, cloud and mist swirling in and out of its crown. A brilliant, jewel-like light often flashes from within the thick shadows of the tree and the people of Suiming rely on this light, scattered from the shadows, for their work and rest.

A young warrior, thinking to improve on the smell of raw flesh, travelling beyond the sun and moon, arrived in the south, saw the light from this tree and thought it very odd. He circled the tree examining it carefully, determined to establish the truth of it. He discovered a bird in the tree, rather like an owl, with long talons, a black back and a white belly. The bird pecked at the tree and a clear, bright fire emerged. Seeing this, the warrior realized how the light was produced. He imitated the bird and breaking off a length of branch from the tree used a small twig to drill into the larger branch. As expected, the light of fire appeared but he saw no flame. He tried again and again with a harder twig and eventually, with continuous friction, sparks flew in all directions and produced a bright flame. He tended this fire carefully and the light of its flames illuminated his heart and the whole world itself.

The warrior spread the skill and experience of making fire to all around him. It was the first time that they had felt such real warmth and light. With its aid, they could see the faces of their relatives and observe flowers, plants and trees and even the ridges of distant hills. Stepping out of their houses they were struck by the sight of green hills and blue water, self and matter were at one. They chased butterflies and imitated the call of birds and experienced a hitherto unknown joy. They gave thanks to this clever young man and followed him voluntarily, calling him "Suirenshi," the man of fire. Suirenshi went on improving the technique for making fire, using different kinds of wood throughout the year; elm and willow in spring, the wood of date and apricot in summer and mulberry wood in the last month of summer; in autumn oak, and in winter sandalwood and japonica. Suirenshi took home the technique of making fire to his own country, spreading the knowledge as he went, benefiting people on the way as his fame spread throughout the world.

The use of kindling for making a fire spread throughout mankind and our ancestors cooked with fire as an aid to digestion. They

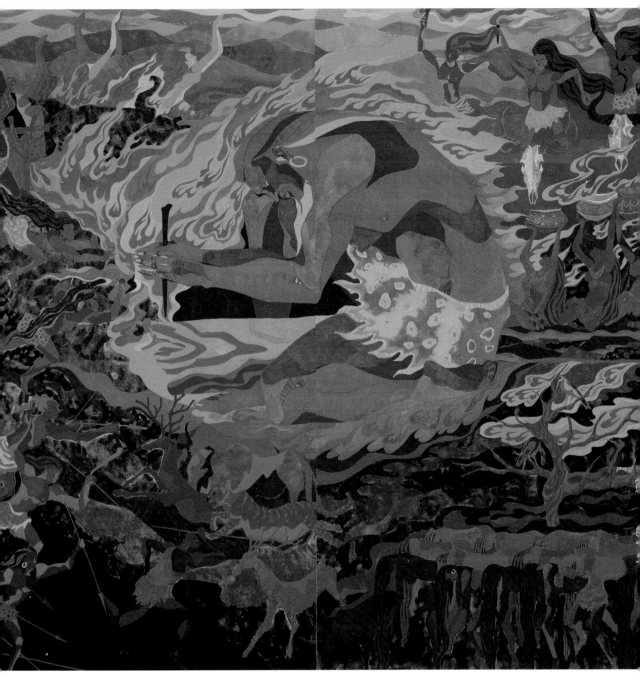

Drilling for Fire
2017
Jia Baofeng (1977–)
Heavy color (*zhongcai*)
Height 166 cm by width 179 cm

used fire for lighting and heat through long nights and cold winters, they used it to drive wild animals into a ring of hunters, they used it to burn grassland ready for plowing, to fire pottery and cast copper, and to refine metal. Fire brightens all.

Suirenshi used a twig to drill a larger piece of wood and after repeated attempts eventually succeeded in producing sparks that became a flame. Firelight illuminated the world that surrounded him and brightened the life of our ancestors. They used fire for cooking, for light and for warmth and they used it to refine metal and bake clay. Fire illuminated civilization itself.

Album: *Ten Thousand Years of the Imperial Succession—Shennong*

Ming Dynasty
Qiu Ying
Ink and color on silk
Height 32.5 cm by width 32.6 cm
Palace Museum, Taibei

THE NOON MARKET

With dwellings and having mastered the use of fire, mankind multiplied more and more and food became more and more scarce. The fruit that man plucked from plants and trees and the plants that he grew did not produce enough. Moreover, not only was there a limit to the number of shells that he could dig from the riverbank, but he was often poisoned out of ignorance and some even died. In those days, those who wanted to eat fish had to dive into the river to catch them, those who wanted to eat flesh had to go to the forests to chase wild animals and those who wanted birds had to catch them quickly when they landed, or climb the tall trees at night with a burning torch to seize them. It goes without saying that man could not swim like a fish, or gallop like an animal, even less could he fly like a bird, so that the chance of catching any of them was pitifully small. Shennong gathered up grain seed, sowed it across the earth and the following year there were cereals to eat. On seeing this miracle mankind then plowed and tended the fields, gathered grain seed and began to plant. From then on, there were crops and the beginning of an understanding about sowing and harvesting.

After Shennong had taught man about crops and planting he also wanted to understand the poison content of each plant so that people would not be poisoned by eating the wrong thing by mistake. In order to do this, he personally tasted all kinds of plants and during his lifetime he established the characteristics of almost all the common plants on earth. From then on, not only were people aware of the poison in plants and no longer died through eating them by mistake, Shennong also came to an understanding of the properties of plants and began to use them to treat sickness. People gradually realized that what was normally a poison could, in sickness, become a medicine and that medicine and poison were mutually interchangeable.

Any kind of invention or creation becomes an exemplar, the ideas that were almost an inspiration such as building nests, the use of fire, sowing and harvest and the use of herbs increased the confidence of the people and became the model for further creativity. In the times that followed, man invented all kinds of new tools, greatly increasing his own physical abilities and increasing the possibility of withstanding the deficiencies and dangers of nature.

Man found it difficult to catch fish and birds; a man called Zhimao made a net modeled on a spider's web. Nets could be spread in the air to catch birds or cast in the water to catch fish. Man could not overtake galloping beasts. A man called Ban discovered that a branch torn from a tree would spring back when bent and thus invented the bow and arrow. From then on, man no longer had to compete in a race with wild beasts; he merely had to practice archery from childhood. People could not swim across very wide rivers until a man called Gonggu

Colored Earthenware Pot in the Shape of a Boat

Early Neolithic Yangshao Culture
Length 24.8 cm by height 15.6 cm
National Museum of China

Excavated in 1958 at Beishouling in Baoji City, Shaanxi Province. This boat shaped colored earthenware pot is a receptacle for holding water and belongs to the class of water pots carried on the person. On the body of the pot, beneath the mouth and between the two ears, there is a mesh pattern in black ink, on each side of the mesh pattern there is a pattern of triangular decorations resembling fish fins. The two ends of the pot point upwards, supplementing the mesh pattern, so that it very much resembles a scene of nets being hauled from the river while fishing, or set to dry on the side of a boat at the conclusion of fishing. The design and patterning put one in mind of fishing boats, fishing nets and the catching of fish aspects of life on the water.

discovered that gourds could float, tree trunks could float on the surface of the water, dried out wood could be fashioned into a boat and flat branches could make oars. From then on man could cross rivers with boats and oars. There was a limit to the weight that the human frame could lift or drag, which made the transport of heavy things impossible. Later, seeing how the Pengcao plant dried into a round shape and rolled hither and thither in the wind, people constructed a round wheel that, after many improvements, developed into the vehicles that we see today.

The growing of farm crops increased the space in which man existed and the tasting of many plants lengthened his overall life. The invention of nets and the bow and arrow developed the use of the hand, the invention of boats and oars and of carts strengthened the function of the foot, and, overall, mankind became sufficient in food and clothing, some even produced a surplus. At this point, it was discovered that what was in surplus in some families was lacking in other families. People then fixed a place where at regular intervals goods could be exchanged and called it a "market." There were no clocks and so it was agreed that the business of the market should take place when the sun was at its highest. When the exchange was over and have and have-not had been balanced out, everybody returned home satisfied and in high good humor with the goods they had exchanged.

Up until this point, man had mastered all kinds of skill and accumulated much knowledge, he now had to find a way of preventing the skill and knowledge from stopping short at the individual and of passing it on to future generations. Obviously the use of knotted cords was not enough.

THE FLAME EMPEROR'S DAUGHTER

When in the prime of life, the Flame Emperor and his wife had their first daughter, known as Yandinu. They kept her at their side, teaching her by word and example; she was clever and eager to learn and anxious to try everything new. The Flame Emperor also had with him the rain master, Chi Songzi, in charge of rain and water. When the weather was fine, Chi Songzi often took a herbal medicine called "Water Pearl" to toughen up his body and, in course of time, he found the way and became an immortal, able to fly up and down freely in a blaze of flame. Yandinu felt grateful admiration for Chi Songzi's abilities and followed at his side, observing carefully, enquiring modestly, and even acquiring the basics of flying heavenwards so that together, the two flew from tree to tree as easily as two birds.

One day, taking his ease, Chi Songzi was taking wine and talking with the Flame Emperor and said: "The affairs of mankind are a complicated mess, more bitter than sweet, why should we so long after it? It would be better to come with me to heaven and live in freedom and happiness." The Flame Emperor gazed at the people of the tribe before him and after thinking deeply for a moment replied: "If we all transcend this world of toil and fly to the heavens, who will support the peoples of the world?" Pointing to some dwellings in the distance he said: "I would hope to live with and among them forever."

Chi Songzi was moved by his determination and realizing that he was in no

mind to become an immortal, knew that there was little that he could say to Yandinu and was filled with melancholy. At a ceremony to pray for rain he ordered that a bonfire be lighted to the side of the altar and when it was over, he bowed deeply to the Flame Emperor, leaped into the roaring flames and slowly ascended to heaven in the billowing smoke. The onlookers stood astounded at this sudden occurrence and Yandinu, who was in the crowd, seeing what was happening, pushed them aside and rushed forward in tears crying: "Take me with you!" In the heavens, Chi Songzi hesitated for a long time, knowing that the Flame Emperor had not wished this. Then set off by the brilliance that surrounded him and without looking back, he gradually vanished into the dark blue of the sky.

After Chi Songzi had gone, low in spirits and without the will to live, Yandinu enquired everywhere for news of Chi Songzi. He now lived in the stone dwelling in the Kunlun Mountain previously occupied by the Queen Mother of the West. His body was as light as a feather and whenever wind and rain drew close, he circled and swooped high and low on the wind above the mountain precipices without a care in the world. But in the shadowless vastness and among the lonely clouds, Chi Songzi would sometimes think of Yandinu at his side and of the despairing look of the sorrow of parting in her eyes as he ascended to the heavens.

In order to follow Chi Songzi, Yandinu redoubled her efforts in the practice of

asceticism and finally succeeded. After a
short period of jubilation, she fell into deep
depression; she could not bear the thought
of leaving her beloved parents but there
was never a moment when she did not
think of Chi Songzi. Eventually she found
a mulberry tree on a mountain not far from
her home and built a nest in it. Sometimes
she changed into a white magpie and flying
home, circled over her parents' house once or
twice, looking at her mother and father and
then returned to her mountain. Sometimes
she changed back into the girl she had been
and paced backwards and forwards beneath
the mulberry tree. The Flame Emperor was
deeply dissatisfied with his daughter. One
day he visited the mulberry tree to urge his
daughter to come home. She immediately
turned herself into a white magpie and sat on
a branch, looking at her father sadly, without
saying a word. The Flame Emperor was much
grieved and in order to induce his daughter to
return to his side, he sent someone to light a
great fire beneath the mulberry tree and burn
down her lodging. The fierce flames leapt
skywards and, in the fire, Yandinu flapped
her wings and, in an instant, she turned into
a white-clad immortal that, like Chi Songzi,
slowly floated upwards on the spiraling
smoke to the edge of heaven.

Tempered in the flames, the mulberry tree
grew stronger still, with a thickness of five
zhang, a height of a hundred *zhang*, branches
that grew out in all directions, red patterned
leaves one *chi* across, yellow flowers and
dark green buds: a tree that attracted even
more chattering birds to build their nests in
it. Yandinu found Chi Songzi in the Kunlun
Mountain and the two immortals became
companions living in carefree mutual joy.

Mural: *Praying for Rain* (detail)

First erected during the Tang Dynasty
Water God Temple
Hongtong County, Shanxi Province

Praying for rain in aid of a bumper harvest was one of the core concepts of water worshipping in Chinese primitive culture. Praying for timely rain in time of drought was a comparatively universal popular belief in China. The depiction of prayers for rain on the west wall mural of the Mingyingwang Hall in the county town of Hongtong in Shanxi Province is a realization of this belief.

At the top of the mural, Mingyingwang (King Mingying) sits on a dragon throne wearing a "heaven reaching" crown ornamented with cloud pearls and clad in a long purple silk gown with a jade belt. His eyes are opened wide as if listening attentively and

he has an extraordinarily imposing and dignified air. In attendance, there are courtiers and handmaidens behind and either side of him bearing banners, parasols and circular fans. Two officials wait respectfully before him, whilst in the center of the steps an official in a dark gown and wearing a black silk cap kneels to present a petition imploring the king to grant the favor of timely rain.

The painting is spacious and figures and scenery are well arranged. All the figures bear different facial features and despite the large number present there is no confusion. Light and shade are also appropriately balanced.

The Emperor's Daughter and the Mulberry Tree

2017
He Xiaowei (1953–)
Lacquer
Height 180 cm by width 240 cm

The Flame Emperor's eldest daughter greatly admired the immortal Chi Songzi, following him through storm and tempest to Kunlun where she later became an immortal as well, living in a mulberry tree not far from home. Sometimes she took the form of a white magpie or appeared as a woman. The Flame Emperor saddened by the forms she took, urged her to return home, but without success. Eventually, the Flame Emperor set fire to the mulberry tree and his daughter at last ascended to heaven.

YAOJI OF WUSHAN

Yaoji, the Flame Emperor's second daughter was an innocent, sad, sensitive girl. When she was a child her paradise had been the garden behind the house where she enjoyed the tinkling of the brook and the warm gentle breeze, spending day after day there, listening to the happy sound of birds and smelling the fragrant scent of flowers. When she was hungry, emerald birds brought her sweet tasting fruit and delicacies in their beaks and when she was thirsty the fresh green grass and flowers provided her with sweet dew. Yaoji and her brothers and sisters could all sing and dance and the garden echoed with her silvery laughter.

Yaoji grew day by day, but pretty as a flower though she was, she suffered from anxiety. She often wept with concern at the

suffering of the people but her heart rippled with love as well; she had a silent fondness for a handsome and intelligent young man, the grandson of the tribal shaman. However, when she was sixteen, suddenly, misfortune struck and she was felled by a grave illness. In tears, Yaoji lay on her sickbed, wishing that she could once more bathe amongst flowers and grass, insects and fish; once more feel the change of spring and autumn, the exit of cold and the arrival of heat and follow her father through the villages and catch sight of that young man at the side of a stream.

With limitless hope and regret for the world Yaoji died before

Handscroll: Copy of Gu Kaizhi's *The Nymph of Luo River* (detail)

Southern Song Dynasty
Anonymous
Ink and color on silk
Height 26.3 cm by length 641.6 cm
Liaoning Provincial Museum

Much praise is devoted historically in Chinese poetry to the Goddess of Wushan that is Yaoji, the goddess of ancient Chinese legend. Song Yu, author of prose poetry in the *cifu* genre in Chu Kingdom of the Warring States Period wrote a prose poem *Shennu Fu*, in which the goddess of Wushan is beautiful, pure, sacred and noble in bearing. Cao Zhi (192–232) of the Warring States Period imitated this work and produced the *Nymph of Luo River (Luoshen Fu)*, in which he described the story of his own encounter with the Nymph of Luo on the banks of the Luo River.

This copy of a handscroll by Gu Kaizhi (c. 345–409) of the Eastern Jin Dynasty (317–420) is divided into three sections and depicts the story of Cao Zhi's chaste romance with the Nymph of Luo. The distribution of figures suits the context exactly, the use of line changes constantly and color is applied with simple elegance. This is one of the treasures of Chinese painting.

her time and those who heard wrung their hands in despair and disbelief. Her father and mother despaired even more and buried her on the sunlit Guyao Mountain amidst forests of bamboo and salsa and surrounded by fresh flowers so that she could continue to enjoy the warmth of the sun and bathe in the blessings of the world. The God of Heaven mourned her early passing, like a flower that had withered before it had had time to open, and appointed her God of Cloud and Rain on Mount Wushan. Unwilling to leave mankind, Yaoji's spirit traveled to the peak of Wushan and became the Yaocao flower of legend. Its leaves grew profusely in layers, the flowers were yellow and its fruit was like cocoons of silk. Any girl that ate the fruit of the Yaocao at once turned into a beauty that inspired love. Growing on Guyao Mountain, the Yaocao flower absorbed the essence of sun and moon and took on human form. But by virtue of standing for a long time on the mountain peak, gazing down on her ancient father and loving mother with limitless longing and inexhaustible love, gradually and unconsciously she was reincarnated as a range of mountains rising amongst other ranges of mountains. One by one, her female attendants also became either large or small ranges of mountains.

In the early morning, Yaoji often turned into a vague misty cloud that floated lazily between the high peaks and deep valleys; in the evening she turned from a cloud into graceful evening rain chattering plaintively with the green hilltops; at night she called out

Handscroll: Copy of Gu Kaizhi's *The Nymph of Luo River* (detail, another part)

The Nine Songs (detail)
Yuan Dynasty
Zhang Wo (?–c.1356)
Ink on paper
Height 28 cm by length 602.4 cm
Shanghai Museum

The Nine Songs are a verse compilation linked with the sacrificial practices of the Chu people. They are based on a set of poems concerning the beliefs in demons and sacrifice current in the Chu lands written when exiled in the south by the poet Qu Yuan. In the part *Mountain Demon*, there is no accepted explanation of the demon but the well-known Chinese author, historian and archaeologist, Guo Moruo (1892–1978), suggested that the Mountain Demon was a version of the legend of the Goddess of Wushan.

This handscroll is based upon the myths and legends contained in Qu Yuan's poem. The Mountain Demon is depicted as naked but for a grass skirt tied at the waist, holding a *lingzhi* fungus and riding on the back of a leopard.

Zhang Wo was a man of many talents, expert in figure painting, who followed Li Gonglin (1049–1106) in simplicity of line, delicacy of brushstroke and vividness of representation.

with deep emotion; the next day she became a floating morning cloud once more. Passers-by sometimes saw Yaoji, cheerless and lonely, and heard her quietly sobbing in the dark. Some had even seen the beauty of her true countenance, heard the tinkling ornaments at her waist and smelled the rare perfume of her body.

Yaoji loved the beauty of the scenery of Wushan and loved, too, the simple laboring people who lived at the foot of the mountain. Every day, she stood atop the towering precipices gazing into the distance and watching the boats coming and going through the gorges of Qutangxia, Wuxia, and Xilingxia, and every day she dispatched several hundred sacred crows with orders to circle above the valleys of the gorges, watch over those coming and going and protect the peace of earth and water.

One year, Ba and Shu were inundated by a huge flood, hardly encountered in history before. Yu the Great was entrusted with the task of taming the waters. Boring through mountains and opening rivers, he came to the foot of Wushan, ready to build

ditches to release the flood. Unwittingly, he angered the toad spirit that had dwelt hidden on the top of Mount Wushan for many years and the toad used magic to impede his progress through the mountain. Yu the Great, caught unprepared, was thrown into disarray. Prompted by the locals he decided to seek the help of Yaoji, the goddess of Wushan. Yaoji admired the fact that Yu the Great did not seek revenge but sought compassion for victims who had been forced to leave hearth and home. She bestowed on him the magic that allowed him to command spirits and demons, and presented him with a heavenly book that controlled wind and water, so that he could subdue the toad spirit and stop the tempest. Later, Yaoji dispatched her attendant ministers to blast a gorge through Wushan to allow the floodwaters in Ba and Shu to escape through the Wushan gorge and pour majestically into the great river.

THE BIRD JINGWEI FILLS THE OCEAN

Nu Wa, the Flame Emperor's youngest daughter, was quick-witted and clever and the Flame Emperor loved her dearly. She was full of curiosity about the world and her mind was filled with fantastic ideas; how high was the sky, how far away was the distance. Whenever she encountered doubt she pestered her mother and father with questions. She particularly liked accompanying her father into the hills on hunting trips, exploring the wild, going to villages and visiting the sick. But her father was busy with affairs and came to the Eastern Ocean as soon as the sun rose and stayed until it set; it was like this every day, and most of the time he could not take her with him.

Nu Wa asked the Flame Emperor: "How big is the sea really? What's the other side of the sea?"

Her father replied: "Nobody knows how big it is, all we know is that it is big enough to be surrounded by the ocean, nobody has ever been to the end of the sea and nobody knows what lies the other side." As he spoke, an expression of yearning and desire appeared in the Flame Emperor's eyes.

Nu Wa thought to herself: "One day, I'm going to the sea to have a look for myself."

One day, Nu Wa was very bored, the Flame Emperor was not at home and her mother was busy. She just had to run down to the sea. It so happened that there were several small boats moored by the seashore. Using all her strength, Nu Wa dragged a small boat into the eastern sea. The further she went from the shore the more excited Nu Wa became. The sea was quiet and calm and Nu Wa floated lightly on the deep blue sea, playing with the fish that leapt from the sea and whispering to the birds that rested on the boat. All of a sudden, a storm arose and the little boat shivered and shook like a leaf in the wind. Nu Wa was terrified but held her breath and went with the storm hoping that she could escape the whirlpool and reach the shore as quickly as possible. The howling wind and rough sea suddenly rose in a rage and a mountainous wave crashed over the little boat, the sea opened its great mouth and engulfed the helpless Nu Wa.

When, after a whole night, Nu Wa did not return, the Flame Emperor and his wife gathered the tribe and searched the neighboring hill forests and seashore for her. They called her name, their sound filled the hills and forests but it was drowned by the crashing waves. When they reached the seashore a tiny bird burst through the waves from the depths of the sea, patterns on its head, a white beak and red claws, calling mournfully: "Jingwei, Jingwei." For a long time, it circled above them, reluctant to leave. In tears, the Flame Emperor said: "This tiny bird is the embodiment of Nu Wa's soul, let us call her Jingwei and hope that her spirit will protect mankind forever." The tiny bird seemed to understand what he said, circled above them three times and then, with a long mournful cry, flew away westwards.

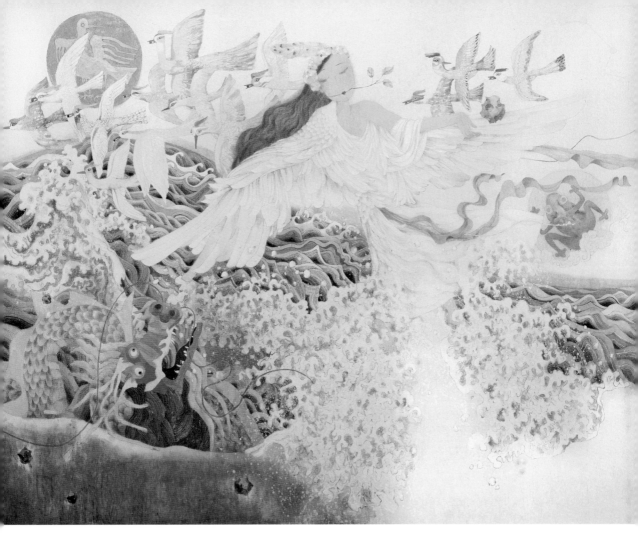

Jingwei settled on Fajiu Hill, calling "Jingwei, Jingwei" every day. She had been destroyed by a cruel and heartless wave and thinking that other young lives might also be snatched away, she decided that the days should not pass emptily by and that she should do something. Flying and calling, Jingwei left the great ocean and returned to Fajiu Hill to pick up stones and twigs in her beak. She picked up and dropped stones in the sea, month after month and year upon year, flying back and forth with neither rest nor stop. Later, a petrel flying across the sea happened to notice Jingwei and was baffled by her behavior. However, when he realized the causes of it all, he was moved by Jingwei's fearless spirit and they became man and wife, raising a large family of birds. The hen birds looked like Jingwei and the cock birds like the petrel. Like their mother, these little Jingwei

Jingwei Fills the Ocean

2017
Ma Xiaojuan (1955–)
Ink and wash painting
Height 315 cm by width 210 cm

According to legend, Jingwei was the youngest daughter of the Flame Emperor Shennong with the name Nu Wa. One day she visited the seashore to play and was drowned in the Eastern Ocean. After death her soul was transformed into a sacred bird with a crested head, white beak and red claws. Every day she flew from the mountains with stones and plants in her beak and deposited them in the Eastern Ocean, emitting the mournful call "Jingwei, Jingwei" as if she were calling out to herself. Even though this is a legend it demonstrates the determination of the Chinese people over the generations to transform nature, unafraid of hardship.

child birds carried stones to fill the sea, day after day and year after year, without rest and without cease.

THE YELLOW EMPEROR BUILDS A CARRIAGE

In the depth of night, Fubao woke with a start at the sound of a clap of thunder outside the window. She opened the door and looked out, a flash of lightning surrounded the Big Dipper, its radiance filling heaven and earth. Fubao suddenly felt a warm current slide through her, she had been struck by the lightning and a strange power shook her body, she trembled with fright and hastily closed the doors and windows and sat up until it was light. A month later she discovered that she was with child, the pregnancy was very long indeed and the amazed tribespeople waited in trepidation for the birth of this curious child. Twenty-four months later, the Yellow Emperor was born. Seen in his swaddling clothes, the ridge of his eyebrows was very pronounced and the bridge of his nose was high, rather like the face of a dragon. He could walk and talk not long after he was born. He was good at observing and imitating and had abilities beyond the ordinary and with the people's support he became leader of the tribe.

Hearing that the central plain was both broad and fertile, the Yellow Emperor decided that he would lead his people to settle there. Burdened with family and heavily laden with supplies, the people moved very slowly and after just half a day's march had to stop and rest. It happened that the Yellow Emperor was resting at the roadside with his people when suddenly a whirlwind blew across the ground, its spiraling wind sucking up thinly rooted straw stems in a bundle that grew larger as it was rolled forward by the wind,

Bronze Chariot and Horses from Emperor Qin Shihuang's Mausoleum No. 2 Tomb
Overall length 3.17 m, height 1.06 m, total weight 1,241 kg
221–210 BC
Emperor Qin Shihuang's Mausoleum Site Museum

This bronze chariot and horses is a half-sized ancient single axle two-wheeled carriage. The chariot and horses are cast from bronze and employ casting, inlaying, and welding in their construction. The chariot and horses are painted throughout with richly colored designs of clouds, geometrical shapes, and *kui* dragons in red, green, purple and blue. In the history of Chinese archaeology, the size, complexity of construction and completeness of harness of this ancient bronze chariot and horses makes it the "crown of bronze."

the more the straws were compressed the more there were. By this time, with the wind as before, an enormous strength propelled this rolling fluffy ball of straw forward and it was not long before it disappeared into the distance. The Yellow Emperor had watched all this attentively and, with a jolt, suddenly recalled that Fuxi had once said that in the country of Qigong there was a kind of saddle that could fly in the clouds, drawn by brightly colored horses and equipped with wheels that was called a "cart." At the time, the Yellow Emperor had paid little attention to what wheels were. Today, however, watching the ball of straw as it rolled over and over, he suddenly realized that this was what it was.

He immediately called for a tool for making pottery that the people carried with them; this was a pair of round wooden plates. The Yellow Emperor took one and gave it a vigorous push down a slope and the now round wheel rolled heavily down. The Yellow Emperor was delighted and promptly ordered his followers to replicate a number of quite large wheels and to remove a space from the center of each wheel to form a round hole, then to connect each wheel with an axle and finally put a wooden box for carrying things on top. The Yellow Emperor gave the wooden wheels a turn and a push downhill and watched them roll down. He was overjoyed. He had solved a difficult problem at last.

The Yellow Emperor had a minister called Hai who suggested that oxen could be used to haul the cart: a curved wooden yoke could be placed across the shoulders of the oxen and a cord could be tied to either end of the yoke, the other ends of the cord could be attached to the cart and the strength of the oxen could then be used to drag the cart slowly forward.

With the use of the cart, the migrating column seemed to grow wings, unleashed arms and legs recovered, the young and old sat on the carts with youths on either side, their happy chatter drowning out the gasping and bellowing of the oxen. Some of the old minstrels on the cart sang and others played, the sound floating away into the far distance.

LEIZU TEACHES WEAVING

On the sixth day of the third month of the lunar calendar, a daughter was born in the family of the chief of the Xilingshi tribe. On the day that she was born a great storm of wind and rain had already blown for three days and three nights. Her father prayed to heaven: "Please give us a sign that will tell us whether the birth of this daughter is auspicious or inauspicious." The shaman performed a divination and pronounced: "Comet and calamity both will come to Xiling at the same time. Unless the comet is banished, it will be difficult for the wind and rain to cease." The leader of the tribe hesitated for half a day. An inauspicious

omen threatened his people and he must decide. Without the knowledge of the family he ordered the shaman to take his daughter to a distant ravine and there cast her away.

At home, his wife searched for her daughter high and low and did not find her. She was broken-hearted but outside, the storm continued unabated and there was no way that she could go out. Her tears fell like rain, she fainted several times and the household collapsed in disorder. Outside, the wind and rain stopped suddenly and the sun blazed. Leading the family, the wife hurried forth in a search of the ravine. To everybody's amazement the swaddled baby was discovered

Below

Handscroll: *Sericulture (The Process of Making Silk)* (the first section)

Southern Song Dynasty
Attributed to Liang Kai (dates of birth and death unknown)
Ink and color on silk
First section: height 26.5 cm by width 92.2 cm; second section: height 27.5 cm by width 92.2 cm; third section: height 27.3 cm by width 93.5 cm
The Cleveland Museum of Art

This long handscroll illustrates the process of rearing silkworms and the reeling of silk from cocoons and the weaving of silk material. It is a precious record of Chinese silk manufacturing technology.

Above

Gilded Bronze Silkworm

Han Dynasty
Height 5.6 cm, circumference 1.9 cm
Shaanxi History Museum

Excavated in 1984 at Qianchihe in Shiquan County, Shaanxi Province. This bronze silkworm consists of nine segments with feet at chest, belly, and tail, all complete. It either has its head raised or is spitting silk. It is finely made and realistically modeled.

According to the *Shiquan County Gazetteer*, in ancient times the raising of silkworms flourished in the area in which it was found. Taking into account the development of the gilding process, the conditions existed for this gilded silkworm to have been a memento or funerary item. The silkworm reeling industry achieved a peak in the Han Dynasty. Large workshops were operated by the authorities, employing several thousand workers and producing gorgeously colored and finely made silks in many patterns. Western Han silks were not only widely distributed throughout China but reached Central Asia and Europe by way of West Asia.

Handscroll: *Sericulture* **(the second and the third sections)**

sleeping sweetly in a tree hole, untouched and unharmed by wind or rain. When she heard the hubbub of people, she woke up and smiled at them. Her smile moved her mother and father and all around. Her mother pleaded with her husband saying: "She

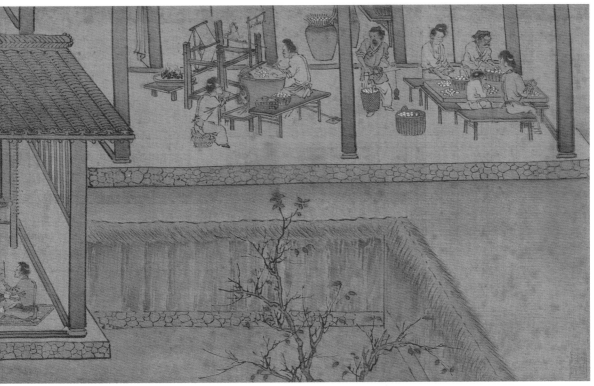

survived the disaster. She's not a portent of calamity but a precious gift from heaven. She cannot be abandoned again!" Her husband was deeply moved and took the child saying:

"We've been settled here for ten generations and this is the first time that we have suffered this kind of disaster. Perhaps fate has involved our ancestors this time. Let us call her Leizu."

Leizu grew up into a pretty, clever and kind-hearted girl. Every day she went out to pick fruit, she looked after her parents and together with her girl companions, sewed all the clothes for the family. One day, she was amazed to see a silkworm on a mulberry tree in the act of spinning itself into a cocoon of silk. She pulled at the white silk, found it tough and light and gathered up some to make clothes for her mother and father. Clothes woven from silk were extremely comfortable, cool in summer and warm in winter. Leizu was inspired to take the silkworms home and rear them, tending them carefully until they spun their silk into cocoons, when she reeled the silk from the cocoons and wove it into silk cloth. All this she taught to other people, holding back nothing. From then on, the people of the country of Xiling no longer wore clothes of bark or of animal skin but were clad in elegant robes of silk and the able and intelligent Leizu became the country's chief.

Between the end of spring and the beginning of summer, the Yellow Emperor and his clan reached the country of Xiling. It had a large population, spread right across a plain between two large mountains. Looking at the lie of the land the Yellow Emperor saw that it would add many miles to their journey if they had to go round. There was no option but to dispatch somebody to the country of Xiling to negotiate, arrange a meeting on the river bank to inform them of the aim of their movement and to make clear that they had no aggressive intentions. In order to mark the solemnity of the occasion, the Yellow Emperor and those of his entourage attending the meeting were dressed in brand-new garments of woven hemp, with deerskin shoes and belts, and jade ornaments hung from their necks. As the spring breeze ruffled the green willows and the lush green grass beside the river, Leizu, escorted by her followers, advanced with measured steps.

Silk

It refers, in ancient China, to natural silk (principally of the mulberry silkworm but also including some tussah silk and silk filament from silkworms fed on tubers). Today, because of the expansion of raw materials for textiles, all textiles woven from artificial or natural long silk fiber can be broadly called silk. However, silk cloth woven from pure mulberry silk is called "pure silk."

The Chinese working people's invention and large-scale production of silk gave rise to the world's first large scale trade and commercial interaction, historically known as the Silk Road. From the Western Han Dynasty onwards, Chinese silk was exported abroad in large quantities and became a well-known product throughout the world. The route from China to the West was known by Europeans as the "Silk Road" and China itself as the "Land of Silk."

As they gradually approached, they attracted the gaze of the Yellow Emperor and his followers. Leizu was young and beautiful, her bearing dignified, but most astonishing of all, her clothing was made from a material that they had never seen before. It seemed of high quality, fine and delicate, like a white cloud floating in the sky. Leizu was much taken with the courteous, upstanding and majestic Yellow Emperor and all talked together amicably.

Leizu invited the Yellow Emperor on a tour of her villages. Outside the door of each and every home in the village there were ranges of sturdy green mulberry trees. On closer inspection they discovered that the green leaves of the tree wriggled with little fat white worms. These white worms were the improved house silkworms bred by Leizu.

Mural: *Zhang Qian's Expedition to the Western Regions*

Mogao Cave No. 323 north wall
Early Tang Dynasty
Dunhuang
Dunhuang Academy, Gansu Province

Zhang Qian (?–114 BC) was a man of an adventurous disposition. In 139 BC, on the orders of the Han Emperor Wudi (156–87 BC), he was dispatched on an expedition to the western regions at the head of over 100 men and opened up the southern and northern routes (the Silk Road) that linked the Han Dynasty with the western regions. He transmitted the culture of the central plain to the western regions and brought back "horses that sweated blood," grapes, alfalfa, pomegranates and pepper as well as promoting the exchange of eastern and western cultures.

This mural depicts Zhang Qian's expedition to the western regions. A palace is depicted in the upper right of the mural with the emperor and officials bearing incense burners paying their respects. At the bottom right, the emperor is seen mounted on a horse with officials in attendance on either side, at the lower left Zhang Qian kneels in farewell. Zhang Qian on his journey is seen on the left of the mural. In the top left-hand corner there is city gate with two Buddhist monks outside and a Buddhist stupa inside. In this picture, Zhang Qian is observed on the march half-concealed by mountains, thus expressing the succession of mountains and rivers to be crossed and the hardships endured by Zhang Qian and his party.

They were larger in size than wild silkworms and spun more silk, and the clothes woven from this silk were even softer, smoother and more delicate. Seeing the look of utter astonishment on the faces of the Yellow Emperor and the others, Leizu burst into laughter and explained: "These are house silkworms that we have raised, we use the silk they produce to make the clothes we wear." She also took them to see all kinds of colored silk materials. The Yellow Emperor was entranced and made his followers note down the techniques for tending silkworms and weaving silk. After several days of contact, the Yellow Emperor conceived a great affection for the capable and intelligent Leizu, while, for her part, Leizu was filled with boundless admiration for this man with all the attributes of nobility that she saw before her.

The Yellow Emperor, after spending night and day in thought, felt that Leizu was the ideal life companion and dispatched messengers to seek her hand in marriage, hoping that the two tribes could join together and become stronger thereby. Leizu accepted with delight. After the marriage, the Yellow

Mural: *Guest Emissaries*

East wall of the middle tomb tunnel of Crown Prince Zhang Huai
Tang Dynasty
Height 185 cm by width 247 cm
Qian County, Shaanxi Province
Shaanxi History Museum

The mural depicts six figures. The three in front are Tang Dynasty officials wearing the court robes of the early Tang Dynasty. They have "basket" crowns, wide-sleeved red gowns over white skirts to the ground, seal cord waist girdles, hold tablets of office and are shod in high court boots and stand in a triangle. They appear serious, poised and confident, and face each other as if discussing arrangements. The three behind are foreign emissaries and the painting ought thus to depict the arrival of a foreign delegation in China. The picture demonstrates the scope and activity of the Tang court's dealings with other nations of the world along the free flow of the Silk Road.

Emperor urged all his clan to learn from Leizu how to raise silkworms and spin and weave silk so that all of them could wear beautiful clothes. As they looked at each other's fine raiment, people realized that there was a happiness outside work.

CANG JIE INVENTS WRITING

In early times, our forefathers used knotted cords or incised marks to record major events in tribal life. By the time of the Yellow Emperor tribal events had increased in number and the use of knotted cords and incised marks often produced errors and was extremely inconvenient. For example, the cords knotted or the marks incised by different people could differ with the person so that it was difficult to know what the actual meaning was, only a general idea was gained and not a precise grasp of

Stone Relief Rubbing: *Figure of Cang Jie*
Excavated from a Han tomb at Yinan, Linyi City, Shandong Province. Cang Jie's achievement in inventing writing had a profound and extensive influence and the occupant of the tomb carved a record of them into the tomb wall. On the left, a four-eyed figure clad in a long-haired animal hide sits beneath a large blossoming tree. Beneath, a plaque reads "Cang Jie." In his right hand Cang Jie holds an object with a handle that appears to have something soft at the end. His left hand is open showing five fingers and he is engaged in conversation with the person opposite.

the matter. Moreover, cord rotted and wood decayed easily. Once spoilt, the exploits of the past disappeared forever. These drawbacks obliged people to think again and find an effective way of replacing knotted cords and incised marks as a means of recording events.

Cang Jie, who had descended from heaven, possessed supernatural abilities and mystic wisdom. He was of elevated character and had four eyes that emitted a mysterious light in all directions. He had a dragon-like appearance and radiated vigor. The Yellow Emperor visited him in the hope that he could invent a new method of recording events. Cang Jie accepted the task and thought deeply about it all day and every day.

One day, when the snow was falling heavily, Cang Jie went out on business and met several hunters. The hunters could look at a footprint in the snow and distinguish which was a deer, or a bear, or a pheasant. Cang Jie had an inspiration; if these footprints could be drawn and issued to the populace, wouldn't it be a way of describing different objects? But, on reflection, if somebody had never seen a bear or a deer, how could they identify their footprints? If you really followed the shape in drawing the image, how would it be possible to depict complicated animals or plants? Even if you could, think of how much time you would waste! Suddenly, he thought of Fuxi's sixty-four trigrams and hexagrams. It so happened that these symbols were capable of representing all things in heaven and earth; why not just use simple brush-strokes to

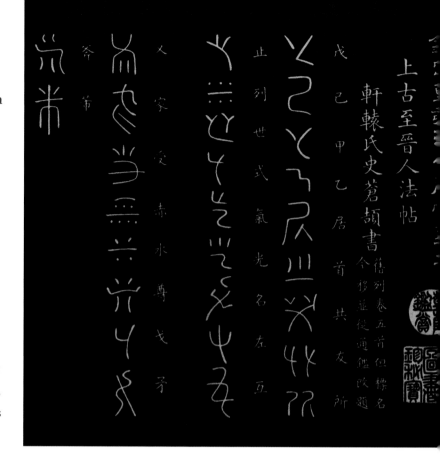

"Bird Foot Script" from the *Chunhua Rubbings*

Legend has it that these 28 characters, popularly known as "bird foot script," came from the tomb of Cang Jie at Shouguang in Shandong Province and represent the form in which Chinese characters were originally created. These curious symbols, formed diagrammatically and pictorially, are, according to legend, the original forms from which Cang Jie created pictogram characters. This illustration is taken from the Cang Jie tablet in the *Chunhua Rubbings* (*Chunhuage Tie*), which placed "Cang Jie script" in the first chapter of rubbings of collected calligraphy.

represent complicated objects? He then set about the process of creating writing on the basis of the form taken by all living things, using the simple to master the many.

In the center of a circle he added a dot to represent the sun, on a representation of the head of a bird he put an eye to represent birds in general, on the basis of the shape of branches on a tree he sketched a few strokes to represent tree or wood, and so on. In this way, Cang Jie and his clan, basing themselves on nature and using simple but beautiful pictures and patterns, created the characters for hill (山), river (川), sun (日), moon (月), ox (牛), sheep (羊), bird (鸟), and man (人). These were called pictograms. On the one hand, he imitated the reality of actual objects to produce a character, on the other, he invested real objects with a meaning. On one level he looked to the circular, twisting form of the *kui* mansion of the White Tiger of the East (the changing movement of the constellations) and at a lower level he copied the patterns on the back of a turtle or the undulations of hills and

rivers, and, on the basis of all these natural phenomena, made sketches on the palms of their hand, thus inventing a written script.

When the news of Cang Jie's creation of a written script spread, it caused a great disturbance amongst the spirits and demons of heaven and earth. The spirits were shocked and, beneath the sky, grain appeared like drops of rain, while the demons were so frightened that they howled half the night. The god of heaven feared that once people were able to write they would abandon agriculture, the very basis of life. Thus, he competed with the trivial benefits to be gained from scratching out characters with an awl. By causing the advance appearance of the grain, first as a precaution against a possible famine and, secondly, as a reminder to mankind not to abandon the bird in the hand for the one in the bush; the demons wept because they feared punishment for their evil deeds noted down in this fearful script. Cang Jie had created a script that had astonished heaven and earth and reduced demons to tears.

Oracle Bone Script

An early form of Chinese characters and one of the styles of the written script. It was incised or written on turtle shells or animal bones and is the earliest discovered documentary record, dating back more than 3,000 years. The earliest examples were excavated at Yinxu in Anyang Municipality in Henan Province. The script looks back to primitive incised or written symbols and forward to the inscriptions on bronze and is a crucial form in the development of Chinese characters. It is the earliest proper systematized script that follows relatively strict rules.

Above
Inscribed Turtle Shell from the Jiahu Site

Neolithic (middle period) Peiligang Culture
6680–6420 BC
Turtle belly plate length 16.2 cm, front width 8.4 cm, rear width 9.95 cm, weight 79.50 g
Henan Museum

Excavated in May 1987 at Jiahu Village, Beiwudu Town, Wuyang County, Henan Province. There is an inscribed mark resembling a human eye and made by a human hand on the rear lower left belly plate. The mark is about 1.2 cm long and 0.3 cm high. This incised mark is the earliest so far discovered in China and may be regarded as a primitive script or as a symbol with all the characteristics of a script.

Below
Earthenware Bowl with Incised Symbols

Neolithic Period
5,000–3,000 BC
Shaanxi History Museum

In the late stages of the Yangshao Culture, many earthenware vessels were inscribed with symbols that possessed a regularity and commonality of character. 38 items were recovered from the Jiangzhai Site and 27 from the Banpo Site. Clearly, these symbols are not mere involuntary scratches and archaeologists consider that, together with the oracle bone and bell cauldron inscriptions, they are an embryonic form of the Chinese written script. They have a particular significance in research into the origins of the Chinese written script.

LINGLUN MAKES MUSIC

At festivals and during their spare time, people enjoyed getting together, blowing through curled tree leaves or tubes of bamboo and drumming on earthenware or iron vessels. There were often pleasant melodies and touching moments and others joined in. The Yellow Emperor felt that melody was not only pleasing to the heart but also had a place in more important events. However, the current tunes were oversimple and too easygoing and he thus dispatched Linglun to produce compositions of harmony and splendor.

To make bamboo pipes, Linglun used bamboo of even thickness from Xiegu on the northern slopes of the Kunlun Mountain. However, when they were played there was neither yin nor yang in the sound, they were basically out of tune and people mocked Linglun, saying that his music was: "Enough to scare wild animals away." Once, the Yellow Emperor was practicing his riding skills and had just got into the saddle when there was the sudden strange sound of bamboo pipes. When the Yellow Emperor's horse heard it, it was so frightened that it bucked, tossing its head and neighing and threw the emperor from the saddle. Linglun rushed to help the emperor, who then said: "It's no easy matter to make a bamboo pipe that can frighten my horse.

It'll certainly produce some good music later."

With the encouragement of the Yellow Emperor, Linglun redoubled his efforts, practicing hard every day but was unable to produce a harmonious sound.

One day, Linglun was visiting Fengling and lay down on a rock, racking his brains when he unintentionally fell asleep. Just as he was sleeping most soundly, he was suddenly woken by the most marvelous birdsong. He sat up at once, rubbing his eyes and looked up to see two beautifully shaped phoenixes with wonderful plumage perched in a tree singing sweetly. Unable to restrain his feelings he took up the bamboo pipe that he had made

Bone Flute from the Jiahu Site in Wuyang

Neolithic Peiligang Culture
Bone
Length 23.1 cm
Henan Museum

Excavated in 1987 from the Jiahu Site in Wuyang County, Henan Province. This 8,700-year-old flute is made from the hollow ulna of a bird. It can play music in a heptatonic scale and is the earliest and best-preserved musical wind instrument so far found in China.

Above
Painted Bas-Relief of an Orchestra on White Stone

Tomb wall decoration
Five Dynasties (907–960)
Length 136 cm by height 82 cm
Hebei Museum

Excavated in 1995 from the Tomb of Wang Chuzhi at Xiyanchuan Village, Quyang County, Hebei Province. This bas-relief depicts an orchestra of 15 musicians and displays the excitement of a musical performance. The first figure on the right is a man, possibly the orchestra's conductor. Twelve of the performers are women, wearing narrow sleeved jackets and long skirts to the ground, who are divided into front and back rows performing on harp (*konghou*), plucked zither (*zheng*), lute (*pipa*), clappers (*paiban*), seated drum (*zuogu*), reeded mouth organ (*sheng*), chimes (*fangxiang*), single reed pipe (*bili*), and side-blown flute (*hengdi*).

Left
Mural: *Band for Dancing* (detail)

Tang Dynasty
Overall length 4.1 m by height 147 cm
Shaanxi History Museum

Excavated in 1952 from the eastern suburbs of Xi'an in Shaanxi Province. Painted on the eastern wall of a tomb, this is the left hand side of an extensive painting depicting a six-man band arranged in two rows. The seated first row is playing lute, reeded mouth organ and bronze cymbals (*bo*), the standing row consists of side-blown flute, clappers and one performer with left arm extended who appears to be singing with a partner.

In looking at this work we seem to be able to experience the pleasures of a musical performance at the height of the Tang Dynasty, the players and singers performing as one in a cheerful and exciting atmosphere.

and imitated the sound of the birds. Just as he was playing at his best, the two phoenixes suddenly stopped singing and flew off.

Every day thereafter, Linglun visited Fengling and sat on the rock waiting for the phoenixes to come and sing. There were always phoenixes perching in the forests of Fengling and Linglun discovered, through long observation, that the call of the male phoenix was strong and elegant and that of the female lingered softly. When a pair of phoenixes perched, each of them first sang six notes, next they called together and then they flew off. Selecting a bamboo with walls of even thickness from amongst the dense thickets of bamboo, Linglun cut a section three *cun* and nine *fen* (about five inches) in length from between two nodules and used it to blow the note known as *huangzhong*. Next, he cut another eleven lengths of bamboo and took them down to the foot of the Ruanyu Hill where he listened to the phoenix calls again and compared them with the *huangzhong* scale to produce the remaining eleven notes. At this point, based on the six-note call of each phoenix and by dint of lengthy study and experimentation, Linglun was able to produce a complete twelve-note musical scale.

Later, Linglun built a small hut for himself at Xiegu where he listened attentively and raptly to every sound of nature. Each different sound, the tinkling of the mountain brook, the soughing of the wind in the bamboos and the singing of the birds, gave him a different impression. Linglun also enriched his melodies by noting down the calls and cries of birds and animals. In autumn, when the harvest was gathered in, Linglun performed all that he had studied and the whole clan found itself immersed in a marvelous natural world, where they seemed to hear all these sounds for the very first time.

Set of Chime Bells (*Bianzhong*) from the Tomb of Marquis Yi of Zeng

Warring States Period
Length of bell frame 748 cm, height 265 cm
Hubei Provincial Museum

Excavated in 1978 from the Tomb of Marquis Yi of Zeng in Beisui County in Hubei Province. There are 65 bells in this set with the largest measuring 152.3 cm in height and weighing 203.6 kg. The set itself has a compass of over five and a half octaves; some bells in the set are tuned to semitones. The scaling corresponds to present-day C major. The set can perform in pentatonic, hexatonic and heptatonic scales. The existence, 2,000 years ago, of such refined musical instruments and broadly based orchestras is exceptionally rare in musical history.

THE GREAT WAR AGAINST CHIYOU

Chiyou was huge, fierce and immensely strong. He had the body of a man but the hooves of an ox, eight pairs of eyes, six hands, any number of brains and teeth two *cun* long, abnormally hard and incomparably sharp. His eighty-one brothers had heads of copper and iron and ate sand and stone. Chiyou was master of the laws of the weather and could command cloud and mist. He held a great axe and his hair stood on end. He had the ability to distinguish between benign spirits and evil demons; no harmful monster dared approach him.

When mountain floods burst forth in the Gelu Hill, the rushing waters carried down vast quantities of silt and swept out copper ore as well. Chiyou and his followers gathered up the copper ore that now lay exposed on the surface and made it into swords, spears and halberds. The floods that occurred in the Yonghu Hill also produced much copper ore, which the Jiuli clans then used to make the halberds of Yonghu and small spears. Leading tribes brandishing these weapons, Chiyou took towns and territory and swallowed up neighboring tribes.

The tyrannical Chiyou fought Yuwang amongst the hills and fields of Zhuolu and conquered all. After defeating Yuwang, Chiyou fought a bitter battle with the Flame Emperor in the same place and the flames of war spread, bringing

Album: *Ten Thousand Years of the Imperial Succession—the Yellow Emperor*
Ming Dynasty
Qiu Ying
Ink and color on silk
Height 32.5 cm by width 32.6 cm
Palace Museum, Taibei

great suffering to the people. Having driven off both Yuwang and the Flame Emperor, Chiyou occupied the territory of Zhuolu. After their defeat, Yuwang and the Flame Emperor sought the help of the Yellow Emperor who raised an army to mount an expedition against Chiyou.

The Yellow Emperor was well prepared for this war. He recruited soldiers from amongst the spirits, invented the bow and arrow and armor, collected copper ore and manufactured the Minghong sword. He trained his army in the battle methods of bears, leopards, tigers and the *pixiu*, an animal rather like a lion. He also made five kinds of banners, a gong with

a handle (*zheng*[1]) and cymbals (*bo*) and drums and whistles with which to raise the spirits of his army. The fortresses of the two armies stood in opposition to each other and their banners flapped in the wind. Both armies took up position, the drums thundered and the shouting shook heaven and earth. No amount of imagination could do justice to the scenes of slaughter. Despite the bravery of his people and their fearless sacrifice and even the rivers of blood, the Yellow Emperor fought a losing battle.

During the fierce and lengthy battles between Chiyou and the Yellow Emperor, Chiyou had deployed his mastery of cloud and mist and encircled the Yellow Emperor so that he could distinguish neither east nor west. In the midst of this all-enveloping fog, Chiyou and his clan appeared and disappeared at will, now here now there, mercilessly

1 *Zheng*, an ancient musical instrument shaped like a narrow bell with a handle and made of bronze. In ancient Chinese warfare drums were used to signal the advance and "sounding metal" to sound the retreat. The "metal" of "sounding metal" refers to the *zheng* in its role in warfare as a tactical signalling device. The phrase "sound the metal, withdraw the troops" (*mingjin shoubing*) originally meant to cease the advance and stop fighting; it has now come to mean complete the task and stop work. The *bo* (cymbal), anciently called *tongbo* or *tongpan* and commonly known as *cha*, is a percussion idiophone used in both Chinese and western orchestras. In ancient China, *tongbo*, *tongnao* or *tongpan*, and *cha*, were collectively known as *naobo*.

Tiger Patterned Bronze *Zheng*

Warring States Period
Musical instrument for troops on the march
Height 39.3 cm
National Museum of China

Said to have been excavated at Xinjin in Sichuan Province. The *zheng* is a musical instrument for an army on the march. It is bell-shaped with a long handle, used with the mouth uppermost and struck with a mallet. It was much used by the states of the south during the Warring States Period. Archaeological studies demonstrate that the *zheng* was still in fashion as a ceremonial weapon during the Han, Wei (220–265) and Jin dynasties. The handle of this specimen is quite long and its body is ornamented with tiger and tree patterns and the script used in the Ba and Shu regions of Sichuan. It is typical of implements used by the ancient inhabitants of Ba and Shu. Ba and Shu were local regimes of the pre-Qin era, Ba in the east of present-day Sichuan and Shu in the west, to the north of the upper reaches of the Yangtze River.

cutting down the Yellow Emperor's panicking troops whenever they encountered them. The Yellow Emperor's losses were heavy but there was nothing he could do. It was at this point that Fenghou, one of the Yellow Emperor's ministers, drew inspiration from the seven stars of the Big Dipper and invented a "Pointing South Carriage." Mounted on the carriage was a small iron figure of a man whose arm always pointed south. Relying on the directions from the carriage, the Yellow Emperor was eventually able to break free and lead his troops out of the dense fogs laid by Chiyou.

Under Chiyou's command there was a band of ferocious mountain and water demon spirits called *chi*, *mei*, *wang* and *liang* who emitted a sound that disoriented the minds of those that heard it causing them to move unwittingly towards the source of the sound where they were slaughtered. Unknown numbers of the Yellow Emperor's troops were confused in this way. Seeing his troops

Mural from the West Slope of Mogao Cave No. 249 (detail)
The detail shows Fengbo and the Rain Master.

attracted towards the enemy, the Yellow Emperor was at his wits' end. Later, one of the emperor's spies reported an important piece of intelligence to him: although the sound emitted by the demon spirits had a mesmeric quality and seemed unbreakable, there was, in fact, an antidote, which was the voice of a dragon. The Yellow Emperor had a magic dragon, the dragon Ying, at his disposal and so ordered it to make a humming noise over the battlefield to counter the sound of the *chi*, *mei*, *wang* and *liang* demon spirits.

By the time that the dragon Ying spread its wings and was soaring towards the heavens, Chiyou had already dispatched Fengbo and Rain Master to raise a storm of unparalleled ferocity that prevented the dragon Ying exercising its abilities. The Yellow Emperor thought of his daughter Ba who lived in the

Kunlun Mountain on the terrace of the water god, Gonggong. Ba had a body brimful of fire and flame and wherever she went, the clouds evaporated and rain dispersed in a great blaze of heat. When she reached the battlefield the wind and rain deployed by Chiyou ceased instantly and was replaced by a blazing heat. Seeing the way things were going, Chiyou was astonished. The dragon Ying took advantage of the situation to deploy his magic abilities and set about killing, taking a number of enemy lives. The Yellow Emperor gained a number of victories in this campaign but was still unable to eliminate Chiyou and his clan completely and their strength remained great.

Faced with an enemy strong in numbers and extensive in territory there was nothing that the Yellow Emperor could do. He saw the falling morale of his own troops and the decline of military strength and was exceedingly anxious. However, he finally hit upon a plan, and that was to produce a particular kind of military drum, the sound of which would strengthen morale and frighten the enemy. The Yellow Emperor had his eye on a wild animal called *kui*, which looked like an ox but without horns. Its skin was gray, it had only one foot and could enter and leave the sea at will. The emperor dispatched

Cloisonne Bowl Inlaid with a Pattern of a *Kui* Dragon

Ming Dynasty
Height 10.9 cm, width at mouth 11.8 cm
Palace Museum, Taibei

The whole bowl is inlaid with a filigree decoration on a blue ground and the belly of the bowl is patterned with a pair of *kui* dragons spitting lotus flowers. The *kui* is an ancient Chinese mythological monster with only one leg. According to the *Classic of Mountains and Seas* it resembled an ox. However, other, more numerous ancient texts refer to it as having the form of a snake and it became one of the major decorative forms, with its long curled tail, open mouth and unsophisticated charm.

The Battle of Zhuolu

2017
Zhang Peicheng (1948–)
Ink and wash painting
Height 313 cm by width 364 cm

Chiyou and his clan fought the Yellow Emperor and his clan at Zhuolu. The Yellow Emperor lost nine battles out of nine but finally, with the help of the Dark Lady, and with cunning military skill and using extraordinary intelligence and stratagems, struck down Chiyou and gained victory.

people to catch one and brought it back, skinned it and used the skin as a drumskin. There was the drum but no drumsticks. The Yellow Emperor then thought of the Thunder God, a kind of monster with the body of a dragon but the head of a man, which often flew in a leisurely fashion amongst the mountain valleys, occasionally striking its belly and producing a sound like a great clap of thunder. To secure victory over Chiyou, the Yellow Emperor sent people to catch the Thunder God and extracted the largest bone from its body to make a drumstick. When all was ready, the Yellow Emperor beat the drum with the bone drumstick, producing a sound louder than thunder that could be heard at a distance of over five hundred *li*. Nine strokes of the drum on the battlefield and the hills shook, the mountains toppled and the earth opened. The Yellow Emperor and his clan rose in triumph. Chiyou and his followers, lost in terror, abandoned their armor and fled.

Despite having been defeated and losing both men and horses, Chiyou knew that if he gave up his weapons and surrendered he would suffer great humiliation. Nobody was willing to be a partner in humiliation and so he made a reckoning of his forces and sought the aid of the giant hominid Kuafu.

Kuafu was a second-generation descendant of the god Houtu. His clan lived on a mountain in the northern wilderness called "the city that carries heaven." Every one of them was huge and strong with a yellow snake hanging from each ear and a snake in each hand. Although they looked fierce, they were actually quite kind-hearted and gentle. They gladly agreed to help when Chiyou arrived seeking aid. Once he had obtained Kuafu's help, Chiyou's morale improved and his military power increased, rather as if a fire on the point of going out had been fed a large amount of firewood.

The Yellow Emperor won none of his nine battles with Chiyou and arrived at Mount Taishan, which was shrouded in a great fog for three days and three nights. There was a woman with the body of a bird and a human head and the Yellow Emperor asked her the secret of victory in every battle and she gave it to him. The woman was the Dark Lady.

From then on, the Yellow Emperor deployed his troops with supernatural skill and his tactics became magical and unpredictable. He amassed the red copper of Mount Kunwu to forge a double-edged sword. This sword glimmered with a cold light, was sharp beyond compare and cut through jade like butter. With a mastery of tactics and the forging of many weapons, morale improved at once.

With two powerful armies locked in combat on the battlefield, it was not enough to rely on sheer ferocity to achieve victory, there had to be some extraordinary stroke of intelligence. Ever since the Yellow Emperor had acquired the skills of the art of war, he had shown myriad subtle changes in the way he deployed his troops and engaged the enemy. By contrast, although Chiyou was fierce beyond compare, in the end he was unable to resist the stratagems of the Yellow Emperor. In the final battle, the remnants of Chiyou's clan and its supporters from the Kuafu clan were tightly encircled by the Yellow Emperor and their attempts to break out finally came to nothing. At this point, the dragon Ying displayed his magical powers and beating his powerful wings came swooping down from the heavens to kill, destroying many of the enemy.

Chiyou and Kuafu's followers were killed and scattered in the surprise attacks of the Yellow Emperor's troops. In the end, Chiyou was taken alive, shackled in chains and put to death at Zhuolu. The Yellow Emperor's men stripped Chiyou's body of its bloodstained shackles and cast them away in the wild. At once, the shackles were transformed into a grove of maple trees where each leaf was bright red. Maple leaves covered the hills, rustling in the north wind like an echo from the battlefield.

THE WORLD OF YAO AND SHUN

One fine day when she was twenty, Qingdu, the daughter of the Emperor of Heaven, went out on a stroll with her family when there was a sudden thunderstorm and, as the others scattered in alarm, she was carried away by a clap of thunder. She became adulterously pregnant by a red dragon and gave birth to the Emperor Yao amongst the winding mountain ridges of the south. When he reached adulthood, Yao was ten *chi* tall with a face that was narrow at the top and full at the bottom. His eyebrows were of eight colors and his eyes were deep-set. He was intelligent and imposing with the appearance of a sage but wizened with worry and rather like a waxwork figure. There were black clouds at the entrance to his dwelling and dragons guarded the gate. He often flew the heavens on six dragons, spying out the land with eyes that could see for ten thousand *li*. On earth, he discovered that the bottom layer of dark brown soil was stickier than the yellow soil above and good for binding together all sorts of shapes and forms. He led his family in digging out this red clay and fired it into the form of

Album: *Ten Thousand Years of the Imperial Succession—Shun*
Ming Dynasty
Qiu Ying
Ink and color on silk
Height 32.5 cm by width 32.6 cm
Palace Museum, Taibei

先君寫此時市四十八歲故用筆設色之精非
他幅可擬追歎當時已六十二寒暑矣藏者其
寶惜之
萬曆六年七月　仲子嘉題

少嘗侍文太史談及此畫云使仇實
父設色兩易經皆不滿意乃自設之
以贈王優吉先生今更三十年始獲
觀此真蹟誠然筆力拉鼎非仇英
輩所得夢見也王稚登題

余少時閱趙文敏公所畫湘
君湘夫人行景設色皆
極高古石田先生命余臨之余謝不歌三十年矣
偶見畫此呈女春頗作唐妝雅秀工而古
態略具因詩滅趙公為此石設色川師錢
舜舉不存無誑精益也附山文微明記

Painted Pottery

Chinese pottery manufacturing techniques may be traced back to the period between 4,500 and 2,500 years ago, typically those of the Yangshao, Majiayao and Qijia cultures.

The vessels of the Yangshao Culture (4800–2700 BC) are mainly of red pottery, followed by gray and black. The principal material is clay though some contain a small amount of sand. The fine clay painted pottery of the Yangshao Culture has its own particular shape, the surface exhibiting a red tinge. Both inner and outer surfaces are polished smooth with some fine patterning. These are the best known of the period. Fine clay painted pottery reflects the standard of the art of pottery manufacture of the time. It has a certain representative quality and the Yangshao Culture is frequently known, archeologically, as the painted pottery culture.

On facing page
Lord and Lady of the Xiang River (detail)
Ming Dynasty
Wen Zhengming (1470–1559)
Ink and color on silk
Height 100.8 cm by width 35.6 cm
Palace Museum, Beijing

Legend has it that after the death of Shun, Yao's two daughters Ehuang and Nuying jumped into the Xiang River and became known as the Lord and Lady of the Xiang River. This painting is the only surviving example of Wen Zhengming's early figure paintings. Lord and lady stand one behind the other, the figure in front holding a feather fan, looking back in profile with an animated expression as if answering the figure behind. The images are elegant and slenderly poised, long sleeves float free and skirts brush the ground. Delineated with a gossamer line and applied vermilion and white, the essence of the whole is one of classical elegance.

Pottery Bowl with Geometrical Designs
Neolithic Banpo-Type Yangshao Culture
Height 16.4 cm, width at mouth 37.4 cm
Palace Museum, Beijing

This bowl has an uneven lip and deep belly with a rounded base (indicating a circular base protruding outwards). Made from red clay, the lip and the outer surface of the belly are decorated in black, the lip with a wave pattern positioned by dots while the belly is decorated with a three-layered triangular geometric pattern, two layers of which are the same shape and size but face in opposite directions. This may be due to the gradual change towards the abstract of the original fish pattern. The construction and patterning of this colored pottery bowl bear all the hallmarks of a classic Neolithic Banpo-Type Yangshao Culture vessel (c. 4800–3900 BC).

vessels and utensils used in daily life, for eating, for amusement or as containers. Yao's outstanding skills as a potter brought great convenience with it and people flocked to learn from him. They also made him leader of the clan.

Yao was frugal, simple in his habits and felt for everybody. He lived in a crudely built hut thatched with untrimmed straw and reeds and with rafters that had the bark left on. He ate coarse grain and drank a soup made from wild plants. In the winter he wore a deerskin and in summer garments of coarse hemp. He devoted himself to the people and regarded their lives as more important than his own. If he saw people who were starving for lack of food, or cold through lack of clothing or in difficulties through error, he always blamed himself and accepted the responsibility as his own, believing that it was he, himself, who had brought suffering on the people. Yao believed in the way of heaven as law and implemented a system of succession through abdication, putting the welfare of the people first. His humanity was heaven sent, his knowledge was god-like, to be near him was to enjoy the warmth of the sun, to observe him from afar was like gazing on clouds.

Yao reigned as emperor for seventy years, earning the deep love and respect of the people. When he wished to abdicate, all suggested Shun as his successor.

Shun had mourned his mother from childhood and grew up into a man with a large mouth and the countenance of a dragon but a small body. Because of years of toil on behalf of the people, his skin had darkened. His four eyes gleamed with intelligence, he wrote with authority and his word was law. He plowed and sowed at Lishan Mountain and before very long the peasants there were transformed by the influence of his virtue and their respect for him increased. He went fishing at Leize and the fishermen of Leize competed to give up their places for him.

Wherever he went he was surrounded by people who listened to his instructions and followed him of their own accord.

Shun had a younger stepbrother called Elephant who was graceless and arrogant. His stepmother was vicious and prejudiced as well. She forced Shun's father to expel him from the home. Several times thereafter the befuddled father and younger brother sought to encompass Shun's death but his superior intelligence enabled him to escape. Shun did not seek revenge and always behaved amiably, his magnanimity spread his reputation far and wide. Wherever he went, local disputes were effectively resolved because of the way in which he had brought the best of virtuous behavior and administration to the locality. Very soon, Shun's words and actions became known to Yao, who, after much observation concluded that Shun was a worthy of a kind rarely encountered and deserving of confidence. Not only did he betroth his daughters Ehuang and Nuying to him, he also abdicated in his favor.

The brutally stubborn Elephant was deeply moved by Shun's brotherly affection. When Shun made a tour of the south, Elephant followed him and tempered by harsh sun and drenching rain, one day took a bath in the Dongting Lake, emerging in totally human form and completely divested of any appearance of an elephant. Thereafter, he cleared and cultivated land at Xiaoshao in the Jiuyi Hill. One day, Shun went into the mountains and was killed in a hand-to-hand struggle with a dangerous giant python at Cangwu in present day Hunan. He was buried in the Jiuyi Hill. Elephant was desolated by the news and changed into an elephant of stone, facing in respect towards the place of Shun's sacrifice. Ehuang and Nuying, Shun's two wives, wept all day, their tears drenching the dark green bamboo so that the bamboo grew to display tearstains. All the virtue of the world began with Shun.

HOUYI ERADICATES THE FOUR EVIL MONSTERS

Four monsters, the Yayu, the Zaochi, the Fengxi and the Xiushe, suddenly appeared amongst humanity slaughtering people, so that wherever they went, none could make a living and there was devastation and depopulation for miles around. On hearing the news, people near and far hid deep in caves amongst the rocks, not daring to gather fruit or to go out to labor in the fields. At night, when they lit fires for light, they did so carefully for fear of bringing disaster upon themselves.

Houyi of the Dongyi Tribe was a brave warrior of great strength with a long left arm and skilled in archery, hitting the target every time. When he learned of the depredations of the four monsters he reported to the god Dijun who presented him with a vermilion spirit bow and a white quiver full of arrows, saying: "Please help the people of the world out of their difficulties."

The Yayu had the head of a dragon, the tail of a horse and the claws of a tiger, its body was four hundred *chi* in length and it could run very fast, its cry was like that of a baby and it was the largest wild animal of all, its victims without number. The Yayu had originally been one of the gods in heaven, who, for some reason had been assassinated by the god Erfu and his minister Wei but had been resurrected by a shaman in the Kunlun Mountain and turned into a monster. Taking the spirit bow Houyi carefully searched for its footprints in the mountains of the west but the Yayu traveled as if flying and was nimble as well. Catching it was very difficult. Houyi searched for days

but found no trace. Eventually, Houyi gave up beating the grass for a snake, drew his bow, concealed himself in a certain hidden spot and waited patiently, immobile and as still as a rock. The birds and beasts in the hills took Houyi for a lifeless stone, passing him by or standing on his head leisurely preening their feathers or even dozing. Several days later, the Yayu finally appeared and at the very moment that its shadow was suddenly passing by, Houyi's long-prepared arrow instantly struck home with a whoosh of incomparable force, and the Yayu expired without even the time to cry out.

Having dispatched the Yayu, Houyi moved on to deal with the Zaochi. The Zaochi, with sharp teeth five *chi* long, carried both spear and shield and would devour a man as soon as it saw one. It was exceptionally ferocious. When it masticated, it produced a "kla kla" noise, as if its mouth was reducing hard rock to instant powder. The Zaochi was bold and fearless and it created an atmosphere of awe and fear wherever it went. Houyi was taken to the pool in the south where it was normally known to come and go, and sure enough, caught sight of its huge figure. The Zaochi, seeing the contempt with which Houyi treated its very existence, at once exploded in rage and brandishing spear and shield, shouting and yelling, it rushed murderously towards Houyi at the head of a black, heavy, whirlwind. Houyi drew a magic arrow, raised his bow and loosed the arrow at the oncoming Zaochi. That swift arrow, truly incomparable in its power, was unstoppable, and in an instant,

smashed through the shield that the monster held before its face, cut through its teeth and penetrated its head, killing it at once.

Having dispatched the Zaochi, Houyi moved on to deal with the Fengxi. The Fengxi was an enormous wild boar of exceptional rapacity that gobbled up everything, laying waste to crops and fruit trees wherever it went. Hearing that Houyi had already dispatched the Yayu and the Zaochi, the Fengxi was uneasy in its mind. Since it had no knowledge of Houyi's magic powers, it plunged ferociously forward the moment it saw him and his bow and arrow. This onslaught was so fierce that, given the huge size of the Fengxi, it was like a mountain falling from the sky. Houyi remained coolheaded and as the Fengxi bore down on him, swiftly leaped aside and whilst in midair fitted an arrow to his bow and shot it into the monster's body. There was a whoosh of white light and it fell to the ground with a bang, the sound of its pain falling unceasingly on the ear.

After the Fengxi, there was only the Xiushe left. The Xiushe was eight hundred *chi* long, the hair on its head was like the bristles of a pig, it could fly in the air and run on the ground, both were places where it scavenged for food and it could be said that its savagery was extreme. It lived on the banks of the Dongting Lake in the southwest and it watched the approach of Houyi fearlessly, despite having heard that Houyi had already dispatched the other three monsters. For a moment, when Houyi observed the terrifying

Houyi Eradicates the Four Evil Monsters
2017
Luo Ling (1981–)
Ink and wash painting
Height 35 cm by width 70 cm

Four monsters, the Yayu, the Zaochi, the Fengxi and the Xiushe suddenly appeared amongst humanity, slaughtering people so that no one could make a living. In a feat of superb archery, Houyi eliminated the four monsters. The people were overjoyed and the world was tranquil once more.

aspect of this monster he felt at a loss, but then thought up a stratagem and pretending to be frightened, turned on his heel and fled. The Xiushe, seeing that Houyi was of a mind to retreat, then took to the air, its bloody mouth wide open, its fire-red tongue sticking out, unwilling to rest until it had slaughtered Houyi. Seeing the monster's tongue flickering towards him like a poisoned sword, Houyi turned suddenly, fitted an arrow and raising his bow, loosed a magic arrow which struck into the monster's mouth and throat like a flash of lightning. There was no time for the monster to turn or roll away and it caught fire, the fire swiftly spreading fiercely so that, in a moment, its whole body was completely consumed and the monster writhed on the ground in agony, a surging river of fire. Only a pile of bones remained of the burnt out monster and this pile became the Baling Hill.

Once these four evils had been removed, the people were overjoyed. Night was now as safe as day, and in gratitude for Houyi's bravery the people told these stories to their children over and over again.

HOUYI SHOOTS THE SUNS

Far to the east of the great ocean there is a place called Yanggu, the valley of the rising sun, where, on a mountaintop, there grows a great hibiscus tree, called Fusang. The Fusang tree grows to a height of several thousand *zhang* and has a thousand girths. It covers the sky and hides the sun as if from the universe itself. The Emperor of Heaven Dijun and the god Xihe and their ten children live here, the ten children being the ten suns born of Dijun and Xihe, all living in warmth and happiness, passing the days in pleasant chatter.

As the dark night draws to a close, the jade pheasant standing at the summit of Fusang stretches wide it wings and begins a call of "wo, wo, wo." As the jade pheasant calls, all the stone pheasants of the mountains and lakes of the world join in and as the stone pheasants call, so the cockerels of every family also join in. In the midst of this sound of calling birds and chickens, Xihe roars by, driving a carriage pulled by six dragons, accompanying one of her sons as he appears

On previous page

Stone Relief: *Thunder Chariot Drawn by a Team of Dragons*

Eastern Han Dynasty
Sichuan Museum

According to legend, each day the sun proceeds from east to west in a
carriage drawn by six dragons and driven by the sun's mother, Xihe. In the
tales of ancient mythology, Xihe is a goddess who drives the sun chariot
and had ten sons with Dijun, all of them suns, living in a Fusang tree by
the sea in the east and taking turns to undertake the daily duty of being the
sun. This stone relief was excavated at Yihe Village, Pengzhou City, Sichuan
Province in 1980 and may be an illustration of this legend. Three dragons
draw a chariot that careers through the high heavens in a flash. The chariot's
wheels present a cloud and thunder pattern in the shape of a whirlpool
and the chariot is escorted by five great shining stars. The chariot has two
passengers, the driver in front with feathers on his/her head being the god or
goddess.

Stone Box: *Houyi Shoots Down the Suns*

Eastern Han Dynasty
Sichuan Museum

Excavated in 1951 at Baozishan, Xinjin County, Sichuan Province. This
illustration on the stone box depicts the legend of Houyi shooting down the
suns. Twin trees occupy the center of the box, with a phoenix perched on
either hand, one male (*feng*) and one female (*huang*), thirteen other birds are
scattered throughout the tree. The *feng* represents the sun and the tree is the
Fusang tree. In the lower left Houyi draws his bow and looses an arrow at
the sun. The picture is vividly realistic and rich in decorative quality.

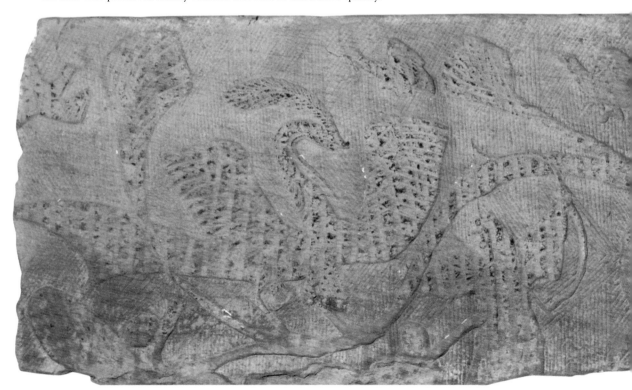

in the heavens, a new red sun leaping from the horizon, splitting asunder the dark night, dispersing the cold and bringing light and warmth to the earth and its people. He travels from the first sunshine to sunset, sinking into the western abyss and returning underground to Fusang where after washing at Yanggu he climbs into the tree to rest. The other nine sons rest and play in the branches of the Fusang tree awaiting the return of their brothers and mother, taking turns by days and months so that the constellations turn and the stars move, solemnly in order and without error.

It would be difficult for ten suns, coming and going, escorted each day in turn by their mother and adhering strictly to a fixed route for a myriad of years, to avoid a certain tedium. One evening, the ten sons of Dijun had a discussion and early the next day appeared together in the sky, playing to their heart's content. Naturally, they burst forth the following day too, gamboling merrily about, freely and without restraint. There was great agitation in the universe as the confused Xihe was unable to control ten healthy, rowdy, obstreperous young children.

How could the world stand ten suns all shining together with neither day nor night? The earth cracked, the lakes and rivers dried up, the trees withered, there was nowhere for humans or animals to hide—behold, the end of the world! Moreover, because of the heat, those monsters, Yayu, Fengxi, Zaochi, Jiuying, Dafeng, and Xiushe, all emerged from the flaming forests or the boiling lakes and using their magic powers slaughtered the people at will. Some tribal leaders knelt at the head of their people and prayed, begging the Emperor of Heaven to rid them of these disasters. Dijun thereupon dispatched Houyi to resolve the sufferings of the people.

After receiving Dijun's command, Houyi, leader of the Dongyi people, took the magic

bow given to him by Dijun and arrived at a great mountain peak, where, standing on two huge rocks, he raised the bow and aimed at the suns in the sky, warning them to stop misbehaving and return at once to their dwelling place. The ten suns did not take Houyi seriously, moreover, as sons of the Emperor of Heaven, did they really need him coming and shouting the odds? The ten of them continued to enjoy themselves and gave forth even more scorching heat, so that the grass and trees of the mountain peak on which Houyi stood straight away burst into flames, covering all in fire and smoke. Tested beyond patience, Houyi loosed off three arrows in succession, each found its target and three great balls of flame fell with a roar into the ocean, one after the other. The remaining seven suns were dumbfounded, but then became enraged and forming a semicircle round Houyi, spouted blazing fire at him. Houyi, angered by their rude behavior, loosed off another four arrows, each again finding its target and another four suns fell to the ocean with a crash. The other three suns fled in fright, but Houyi fitted an arrow, caught up with a fleeing sun and shot him down in an instant. Seeing another sun about to flee, another arrow and another blazing ball fell to an ocean already set aboil by their flames. As he fitted another arrow,

Lacquer Box from the Tomb of Marquis Yi of Zeng

Warring States Period
Hubei Provincial Museum

The lid of this wooden clothes chest is painted with two scenes representing Houyi shooting down the sun (top and bottom right).

Houyi realized that only one sun remained. He hesitated a moment and suddenly heard people shouting: "Houyi, leave us the last sun! Shoot it down and there will be darkness forever!" Houyi looked at the last lop-sided sun trembling with fear, put away his bow and sheathed his arrows and sat wearily down on the mountaintop. He was covered in burns. The people looked at him from afar, cheering enthusiastically and calling his name. The sound covered the earth as if celebrating the arrival of rain and the beginning of days of peace.

The nine suns that had been shot down did not die, they remained the children of Dijun and Xihe and after this short rebellion returned to their mother and father and after seeking forgiveness went back to the Fusang tree, where, year upon year the days and months passed in order and time was constant, a perpetual test. That brief rebellion now seemed more like flames that had obstructed the passage of normal time.

CHANG'E FLIES TO THE MOON

There were twelve moons born to Dijun and Changyi, of whom one daughter was named Chang'e. She had hair that fell like a black waterfall, was sweet and good-looking, could dance and sing and was the apple of her parents' eye. In shooting down the suns, Houyi had achieved a miracle and earned the love and respect of the people. Dijun betrothed Chang'e to him and the pair lived together in harmony. Apart from passing on his skills and hunting, Houyi spent all day with Chang'e and people envied the sweetness of their life.

Houyi was good-natured and always conscious of the suffering of those around him. Hearing of a magic spell of the Queen Mother of the West, that could free mankind from all disasters, man-made or natural and from old age and death, he determined to seek a meeting with her and plead for her help. The Queen Mother of the West had the tail of a leopard and the teeth of a tiger. She was skilled in whistling up and

The Moon Goddess Chang'e
Ming Dynasty
After Tang Yin (1470–1523)
Ink and color on paper
Height 136.2 cm by width 58.7 cm
Metropolitan Museum of Art, New York

Chang'e stands in a gentle pose with her skirt and girdle drifting in the breeze and holding an osmanthus blossom. Her head, in particular, is amply and fluently delineated and suitably and completely expresses her elegant beauty. The face is treated with a pure lunar-white wash that shines as bright as moonlight.

managing the demons of pestilence. She was attended by three birds of prey with dark bodies, red heads and black eyes who could, on an instant, fly a thousand *li* over hills and mountains to bring her sumptuous food. Sometimes, she would stand on the edge of a precipice, and, raising her head to the sky, whistle loudly with a long-lasting sound that filled the hills and valleys and frightened the animals, causing them to flee for their lives. The Queen Mother of the West commanded the demons of pestilence, and could both unleash disease or drive it away and take lives or save them. She had discovered a tree that flowered once in a thousand years and bore a mere handful of fruit a thousand years after that. She plucked this fruit and

Stone Relief: *Image of the Queen Mother of the West*

Eastern Han Dynasty
Length 45.5 cm by width 40.3 cm
Sichuan Museum

Excavated in 1955 at Qingbaixiang, Xinfan Town, Xindu District, Chengdu, Sichuan Province. The Queen Mother of the West, in wide sleeves, sits on a dragon tiger throne in the very center of the picture, surrounded by a toad dancing upright, a nine-tailed fox, a jade rabbit holding a *lingzhi* fungus, a three-footed bird and human figures paying their respects.

from it distilled an elixir of life that became her greatest treasure. People in their hundreds of thousands searched for traces of the Queen Mother of the West in the hope of acquiring this elixir. But the Queen Mother of the West was of no fixed abode, sometimes she lived at the Jade Lake at the summit of the Kunlun Mountain and sometimes at the Jade Mountain to the west of Kunlun. At other times she lived on the Yanzi Mountain where the sun sank beneath the hills, moreover, a bottomless abyss lay at the foot of the Kunlun Mountain and a fierce fire blazed beyond it, so that ordinary people found it difficult to approach.

The moment the news that the Queen Mother of the West lived in the Kunlun Mountain reached him, Houyi at once set out on his quest. Relying on invincible willpower, intelligence and knowledge, Houyi crossed the encircling waters and the fiery obstacles and reached the Queen Mother of the West at the Jade Lake. The Queen Mother of the West was completely aware of Houyi's achievements and admired the contribution

Rabbit with Osmanthus Tree in the Moon (detail)

Qing Dynasty
Jiang Pu
Ink and color on paper
Height 99.3 cm by width 43.5 cm
Palace Museum, Beijing

The full moon is brushed in ink with the jade rabbit appearing lively and attractive. The leaves and branches of the osmanthus tree are delineated in ink with the blossom touched in orange, adding a touch of warmth to the chill of the moon palace. The composition is tightly organized and ink and color deployed with great skill.

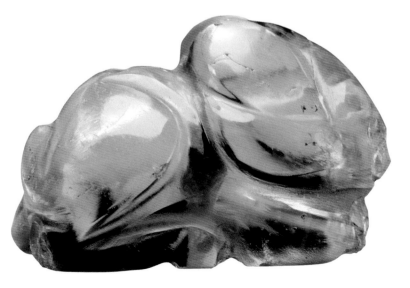

Crystal Rabbit

Southern Song Dynasty to Jin Dynasty (1115–1234)
Palace Museum, Taibei

The Jade Rabbit is the rabbit of ancient legend that lives in the moon with Chang'e and helps her pound the elixir of immortality. In Chinese culture the rabbit is not only one of the twelve zodiac animals but also one of the elements of the Mid-Autumn Festival, representing the hopes of all people for family reunion on the night of the full moon. The Jade Rabbit has always been regarded as auspicious.

The Eighth Month from a Compendium of the Twelve Months

Qing Dynasty
Anonymous
Ink and color on silk
Height 175 cm by width 97 cm
Palace Museum, Taibei

Scholars believe that this work may have been a co-operative venture painted by different painters from palaces in the early Qianlong reign. It depicts the twelve months of the lunar year by season—spring, summer, autumn and winter—according to folk festival and custom. It is painted in meticulous detail and fine color, the perspective is correct and each painting of the set contains human figures, terraces, pavilions and buildings, giving the feeling of a kind of heaven on earth. The courtyard structures extend from the lower left or right-hand corner of the picture into the distance and two or three groups of people appear here and there engaged in seasonal activities.

This work depicts the night of the full moon at the Mid-Autumn Festival. People are standing on the terrace, preparing a banquet or gazing at the moon, a scene of joyful harmony.

that he had made. Houyi explained his quest and the Queen Mother of the West ordered her magic bird to fetch a gourd from the lacquer black cave which she then gave to Houyi, telling him that it contained enough elixir for two people to live forever, but if only one person took it, there was also a hope of living in heaven as an immortal.

Houyi could not think of abandoning his wife and took the elixir home, giving it to her to keep. Chang'e put it in a jewel box on her dressing table.

After having shot down the suns, Houyi's fame spread far and wide and many aspirants came seeking instruction. Mixed in amongst them was one called Pangmeng, a man who followed Houyi everywhere and knew everything about his movements and activities. By chance, he had seen Houyi handing Chang'e a beautiful box, and through careful observation had established that it was the elixir of life. One day, when Houyi was out with his followers hunting in the hills, Pangmeng feigned illness and remained at home. Waiting until Houyi had left, he then threatened Chang'e with a sword and demanded that she hand over the elixir. Chang'e knew that she was no match for Pangmeng and, in danger, opened the jewel box and swallowed the elixir. In a moment, her body floated lightly through the window and flew straight to the Moon Palace. As she ascended she looked back at mankind, the mountains and rivers and the trees and grass, all receding further and further into the distance and the clear skies and a lonely palace became her final garden.

That night, when he returned home, Houyi discovered the box lying on the ground and the weeping maidservants told him what had happened during the day. It was too late for Houyi to do anything and Pangmeng had already fled. Each month on the day of the full moon, Houyi spread the fresh fruit and delicacies that Chang'e liked

The Mid-Autumn Festival

It falls on the fifteenth day of the eighth month in the lunar calendar, a traditional festival celebrated by many nationalities in China and throughout the nations of the Chinese cultural circle. The festival customs of moon sacrifice, admiring the moon, moon worship and eating mooncakes and drinking sweet osmanthus wine originated in ancient times and have continued unbroken until the present. The roundness of the moon at the Mid-Autumn Festival is a treasured and colorful cultural legacy that is a harbinger of reunion and a guardian of thoughts of home and of relatives. It also represents a longing for a good harvest and happiness. The Mid-Autumn Festival stands with the Dragon Boat Festival, the Spring Festival and Qingming, the sweeping of graves, as one of the four traditional Chinese festivals.

to eat in the rear courtyard and drank alone to the moon. The shadows of the flowers swayed and the trees quivered in a gentle breeze, as if Chang'e could be seen dancing alone in the Moon Palace. After she had fled to the moon, Chang'e, together with a toad that was already living there, controlled the movement of the moon and together with a white rabbit she managed the progeny and affinities of mankind. Chang'e, the toad, and the rabbit depended each upon the other. Day and night, they pounded the sweet osmanthus on the moon into a fairy medicine and when the sweet osmanthus flowers floated their fragrance on the air, the seeds fell to earth. Then the moon shone bright and fragrance filled the earth like a shadow of the traces of love.

BOGUN RECEIVES ORDERS

It is said that when Emperor Yao wielded power in the Kunlun Mountain, there was a great flood. Bogun, a young man who had just been ennobled as lord of the rivers and who lived in the uttermost depths of the Less-than-Whole Mountain, received orders to control the floods.

He hurried off to find his father Luoming to discuss his grandfather, the Yellow Emperor's stories of the first great flood. "Who, amongst you death-bound half-spirits can remember the fury of the heavens?" After enumerating the previous evils of mortal life and the actions of the troublesome spirits, Luoming said: "And after forty days and forty nights of rain, there was no difference between land and sea, the evil and the innocent too had all gradually sunk and perished and there was a deathly stillness on the waters. Only the two purest people had survived, a man and a woman. The gods had hoped that through this cataclysm they could create a wonderful new mankind, unlike the very earliest man."

Bogun listened and said: "Isn't that rather too violent? You always taught me that there was no humanity, either in heaven or on earth and I know that to talk of humanity and violence with the gods is absurd. But, honored father, how can the gods guarantee that having once flattened everything, the process of re-construction that follows will not contain the slow seeds of fresh corruption? When you look at mankind now, do you not see the evils you have just

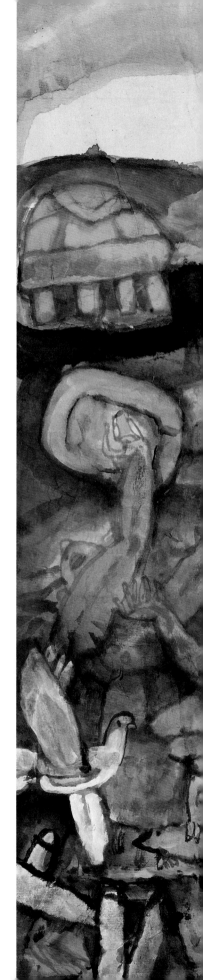

Bogun Devotes His Life to Controlling the Water
2017
Shi Dawei
Ink and wash painting
Height 40 cm by width 41 cm

Bogun was ordered to control the waters and sucked up the floods that covered the land, just leaving a few streams and lakes. As soon as they saw that there were no more floods, people who had sought refuge in the mountains descended to the plains and started work once more. Bogun was satisfied with his work. However, he gradually began to realize that the way he had gone about things would only lead to even greater disaster and could not solve the basic problem.

described occurring as before? And if, at this moment, the gods are intending some fresh disaster, what can possibly be the significance of the work that I am about to undertake?"

Luoming merely replied: "Because you are now lord of the rivers. You receive the sacrifices of the people and the commands of the gods."

Bogun set forth, ascending through darkness and silence.

The first thing that he saw was a sky full of stars. Then he saw two new moons, a faint yellow one hanging in the distant sky and another, a pale white, above the waters. Penetrating the clouds of dark blue smoke, he made out vague bonfires amongst the mountains, lit by the crowds of people forced up into high ground by the rising floods. Taking into account his gigantic stature it could be said that the water never rose above his knees. He carefully avoided the great sharp tree branches that sometimes flashed passed him like torpedoes, striking the rocks with an ear-splitting sound.

Bogun found a level, more or less dry, terrace high up and sat down, thinking of what he should do next. The sky was gradually brightening and the pink clouds of dawn were gathering in the east, a beauty that he had never before experienced.

Later, the people who had emerged that morning from caves, caverns, holes and nests recalled that in the faint light of dawn they had seen a gigantic horned yellow animal leaning down as if sipping from the water so that the mud, trees, and rubble covered by the water had completely reappeared at last. However, when they had dashed back to call the others to come and look, all there was to see was brilliant sunshine and stretch after stretch of ground covered in pools that looked as if they had just been pumped dry.

Humans can never see gods because gods have the ability to conceal themselves at will. Demi-gods are the same. However, because demi-gods have certain human characteristics they sometimes forget their shape and this is what had happened to Bogun when he had first seen the sunrise.

Thereafter, Bogun was careful not to let mankind discover him again. He sucked dry the floods over vast spaces of land leaving a few streams and lakes, and then levelled the surrounding mountains a little to block the distant waters, thus forming a number of large and small basins. When people hiding in the mountains saw that there were no more floods, they came down and started to labor in the plains again. Bogun was well satisfied with his work and bit by bit moved eastwards.

The mountains relaxed in shape and the plains grew. Bogun felt his strength somewhat over-taxed. Because of the extent of the space involved, the rocks of the surrounding mountains were not enough to block the water and he had started by depending on the power of his legs to return to the Less-than-Whole Mountain and the Chongwu Mountain next door to gather stone. He had soon discovered, however, that as far as those boundless eastern plains stretching invisibly into the distance were concerned, the stone that he had carried a thousand *li* was of no use whatsoever. The floodwaters stretched to the sea and the sea, swollen by melting glacier water, rose and powered by the tide, came pouring in to join the recklessly surging rivers. He was merely lord of the rivers, he did not have the strength to suck the sea dry, nor was it permitted.

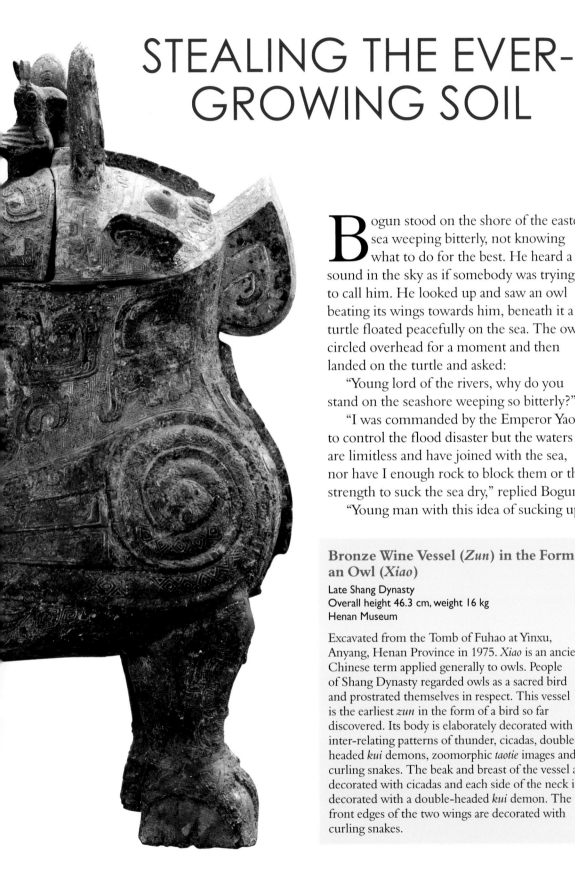

STEALING THE EVER-GROWING SOIL

Bogun stood on the shore of the eastern sea weeping bitterly, not knowing what to do for the best. He heard a sound in the sky as if somebody was trying to call him. He looked up and saw an owl beating its wings towards him, beneath it a turtle floated peacefully on the sea. The owl circled overhead for a moment and then landed on the turtle and asked:

"Young lord of the rivers, why do you stand on the seashore weeping so bitterly?"

"I was commanded by the Emperor Yao to control the flood disaster but the waters are limitless and have joined with the sea, nor have I enough rock to block them or the strength to suck the sea dry," replied Bogun.

"Young man with this idea of sucking up

Bronze Wine Vessel (*Zun*) in the Form of an Owl (*Xiao*)

Late Shang Dynasty
Overall height 46.3 cm, weight 16 kg
Henan Museum

Excavated from the Tomb of Fuhao at Yinxu, Anyang, Henan Province in 1975. *Xiao* is an ancient Chinese term applied generally to owls. People of Shang Dynasty regarded owls as a sacred bird and prostrated themselves in respect. This vessel is the earliest *zun* in the form of a bird so far discovered. Its body is elaborately decorated with inter-relating patterns of thunder, cicadas, double-headed *kui* demons, zoomorphic *taotie* images and curling snakes. The beak and breast of the vessel are decorated with cicadas and each side of the neck is decorated with a double-headed *kui* demon. The front edges of the two wings are decorated with curling snakes.

the sea, may I ask what happened to the water that you sucked up from the land, where did that go?" asked the owl.

"I blew it into the clouds and the cloud god gave it to the oceans," said Bogun.

"So, even if you could now suck up all the water of the sea, where would you put it?" the owl continued.

Bogun felt not only useless but stupid as well. He then asked the owl, saying: "Oh, wisest of all birds, tell me, please, what to do."

"I hear that all things depend the one upon the other, both for and against. I've also heard that in the Kunlun Mountain there is a substance called ever-growing soil that is against water, it looks like clay and expands when it touches water and it never shrinks. Were you to obtain some, there would be no fear that the floods would not recede, however ..."

"However, what?" Bogun asked.

"Let's go," said the hitherto silent turtle.

The owl nodded and treading fiercely on the turtle's back, opened its wings and leaped into the air. The tortoiseshell colored turtle at once sank into the sea.

In the following days, Bogun continued to wonder what this "ever-growing soil" was, the lack of detail in the owl's description having increased his curiosity several-fold. In the end, he decided that he would first pay a visit to the Kunlun Mountain. The documentary record does not say how Bogun obtained the ever-growing soil, merely that he stole it. Perhaps he first sought permission from the Emperor Yao who refused, and then impetuously took it upon himself to somehow steal it. The guardian gods very quickly reported the theft to the emperor, but because of Bogun's status as the grandson of the Yellow Emperor, no pursuit was mounted. In fact, had it not been for the arrival of Bogun, the Emperor Yao would have forgotten that there was this treasure

in the palace dating from the time of Nüwa, the power of which he now wanted to see for himself.

Bogun took the lead in sprinkling the ever-growing soil in the plains and along the seashore. He watched the magical soil fall into the water and then swell rapidly so that a vast body of water quickly grew into an area of wetland and then turned to dry land. The devastating waters of the past were either trapped underground by the soil (forming what we now know as groundwater), or driven, drop by drop, into the ocean.

He felt extremely happy. But he very soon saw that the shoreline was receding, places that had been home to a flourishing marine life were being filled in by the breathing mud of the ever-growing soil. A large number of fish and prawns that had not been quick enough to escape to the depths of the ocean now lay gasping and struggling for breath on the rising and drying mudflats. Moreover, lakes and rivers of all kinds were gradually drying out because of the action of the ever-growing soil, crocodiles and frogs had been forced to take to the forests and the soil was expanding at an unimaginable rate. He wanted to take back the ever-growing soil but it was already everywhere and, like an epidemic, difficult to eradicate.

The Mystic Turtle (detail)
Jin Dynasty
Zhang Gui (dates of birth and death unknown)
Ink and color on silk
Height 26.5 cm by width 53.3 cm
Palace Museum, Beijing

The sacred turtle and the dragon, phoenix and *qilin* are known as the "four sacred animals." The turtle has always been regarded as an auspicious representative of long life and as the common animal totem of Chinese mythology. The turtle's head raises and a puff of vapor escapes its mouth. A red sun (containing written characters) appears amidst the auspicious clouds and the picture is infused with an air of great mystery.

Bogun knew that he had made a mistake so great as to be cast in bronze and went to the Weiyu Mountain to await the punishment of the Emperor of Heaven. Here, in the darkness of the north pole, where the sun never shone, a candle dragon stood guard, a candle in its mouth. Bogun waited in the candle's gloomy light.

Zhurong, the fire god, his ears pierced with snakes of fire, soon arrived from afar on the back of a fire dragon.

"You know why I'm here, Bogun," said Zhurong in midair.

"I do," replied Bogun.

"Some gods, for example Xishi and Heshi, have pleaded in your defense, saying that for years you have toiled to control the floods, distinguishing neither day nor night, winter nor summer. But the gods of four hills and the gods of the sea are unwilling to let the matter drop, they accuse you of destroying the mountains and attempting to fill the sea for the benefit of mankind, leaving many mountain elves and sea dwellers homeless."

"They are quite right."

"Also, the Emperor Yao is furious. You ignored advice and stole the ever-growing soil, this is a great crime; ignorant of the proper way of doing things and in vain, you brought fresh disaster to mankind in place of the old. This crime cannot be pardoned."

"How is mankind now?" asked Bogun.

"The flood may have receded but there is a great drought and naked earth stretches far and wide. The ever-growing soil continues to spread and the sea is shrinking."

Bogun fell silent.

"Only the sacrifice of the blood of the guilty god will turn back the ever-growing soil." Zhurong paused and then said: "Although you are of noble birth and a descendant of the Yellow Emperor, you are not exempt from obedience to the unshakeable law. Young lord of the rivers, have you anything more to say?"

Bogun asked: "I would like to know, if the supreme god did not intend to destroy mankind once more, why did he visit it with a flood so difficult to resist? And why he wished me to undertake a task that could never be completed?" As he asked, Bogun suddenly realized that this was what he had asked his father, Luoming, at the time.

"This question is beyond my competence,"

Bronze Mask with Far-Seeing Eyes

c. 1700–c. 1200 BC
Height 66 cm, width 138 cm
Sanxingdui Museum, Sichuan Province

Excavated from No.2 Sacrificial Mound at Sanxingdui. There is an oblong hole in the forehead of this mask and the ears have the shape of a pointed peach and the appearance of flying. The eyebrows are raised and the eyes slanted. The eyeballs extend outward in the form of a tube for 16 cm. The bridge of the nose is high and the mouth wide and deep with a mysterious smile.

In ancient mythology there was a heavenly candle dragon that controlled light and dark in heaven and earth. "Straight eyeballs" was one of the characteristics of its appearance. The construction of this mask makes it likely that it has some connection with the candle dragon described in ancient records.

sighed Zhurong and forthwith killed Bogun. At the very moment that Bogun's fresh blood spurted forth, the ever-growing soil, that had been spreading unchecked, stopped at once, like a waterfall suddenly frozen in midair.

THE SPIRIT'S JOURNEY TO THE WEST

Though Bogun's body had fallen to the ground, the burden of guilt, remorse and regret that he carried prevented him dying on the spot and his spirit was transformed into a yellow bear, determined to return to the hills of Xuanyuan and get to the bottom of it all with his grandfather, the Yellow Emperor. He traveled northwest, passing through the wilds of Liguang and meeting the ten gods created from the intestines of Nüwa who lay happily across the road. He journeyed on as the sun and moon rose in the east and set in the west, through the Yumen Mountain of Fengju, the mountains of Aoaojushan, Longshan, and Fangshan and past the mountains of the Sun and Moon where a god called Wheeze who had a human face, no arms, and legs crossed over his head, stood guard. He crossed the

Mural: *Greeting the Original God of All* (detail)
Yuan Dynasty
Ma Junxiang and others (dates of birth and death unknown)
Height 4.26 m by length 94.68 m
Hall of the Daoist Trinity (*Sanqing Dian*), Yongle Palace, Shanxi Province

This mural depicts the story of the assembled gods greeting the Original God of All (*Yuanshi Tianzun*). The picture is a detail from the west wall and shows a dignified and kindly Queen Mother of the West, seated in the center wearing a phoenix crown and ceremonial robes, with officials on either side. The Queen Mother of the West is a major figure in Chinese mythology and in this portrayal she no longer resembles the figure from the *Classic of Mountains and Seas*. Her face and figure are full in the Tang Dynasty tradition of ample beauty.

Mural from the South Slope of Mogao Cave No. 249 (detail)

Western Wei Dynasty
Dunhuang
Dunhuang Academy, Gansu Province

This cave was constructed during the late Northern Wei (386–534) and early Western Wei dynasties. The central ceiling boss is painted with hanging lotus, flames, honeysuckle and lotus blossom. The painting of the Queen Mother of the West on the south slope differs from the description recorded in the *Classic of Mountains and Seas*. Here, she wears her hair in a high bun and is clothed in a wide sleeved gown. She drives a chariot drawn by three phoenixes preceded by an immortal also riding a phoenix. The chariot is covered by a colored canopy that floats behind in the wind and flying Apsaras accompany her fore and aft of the chariot. The forests beneath are painted with goats, wild oxen, ravenous beasts and feathered humans.

mountains of Changyangshan, where the head of Xingtian, who is said to have fought for supremacy with the Yellow Emperor on this spot and been decapitated, is buried. Thereafter, shield in one hand and axe in the other, he threw himself into the fight using his nipples as eyes and his navel as a mouth. Finally, the yellow bear crossed the mountains of the great wilderness where dwelt the son of Zhuanxu who had one arm but three faces and was immortal. He passed the country of husbands and the country of wives and arrived at the wilds of Dawo, the land of fertility, where everything that gods or men desired was available in abundance, where phoenixes danced and sang and all the animals gathered. The Queen Mother of the West, the lord of Dawo, welcomed him with a banquet and asked after the reason for his visit.

"I'm just passing through on my way to my grandfather the Yellow Emperor in the hills at Xuanyuan to get an answer from him on a matter between myself and the gods. He is the supreme god and knows all," said Bogun.

"That's true, the god's power is limitless," said the Queen Mother of the West, "but he doesn't concern himself with each and every answer, child, he's just there, ordering affairs according to some unfathomable intention. Your grandfather may pay you no attention. Besides, he's fathered so many children who've fathered so many grandchildren. From your point of view, he's your only grandfather but you're not his only grandson."

"Then what should I do?" asked Bogun.

"Mortal demi-god, you'd be better off staying here, you'll find many companions. To start with they were all like you, full of resentment difficult to assuage, but having once reached this paradise ... they found that paradise has the wonders of paradise and they have become the cynosure of all eyes."

"They're not in mental anguish anymore?"
"Never again."
"But what about the things they never

finished? And the problems they could never solve even if they died?"

"They never think of them."

"But I couldn't do that," Bogun began to weep. "I spent years of effort trying to control the floods. I took great risks in stealing the ever-growing soil. I'd wanted to save people and as a result ... it's too ridiculous. I feel my life's a joke. There's no way that I can spend my time in your country laughing, burdened by such a joke."

"Very well, my child, I won't force you. Go. Go and find your grandfather and if you see him, give him my regards. If you don't see him, there's a mountain called Lingshan to the south, where there are ten shamans, they may be able to help you," said the Queen Mother of the West in conclusion as she dispatched one of her red-headed, black-eyed dark birds to guide him on his way.

Bogun's spirit bade farewell to the Queen Mother of the West and continued on its way, accompanied by the dark bird. There were many strange sights to be seen en route, for example the racoon-shaped dragon fish and the Chenghuang in the form of a fox with horns on its back. It was said that whoever was able to ride on its back would live for two thousand years. Early in the morning they arrived at the foot of a hill. The dark bird told Bogun that the hill was called Qiongshan and that the hills of Xuanyuan lay the other side. The dark bird then flew off, leaving Bogun at the foot of Qiongshan.

Bogun was delighted, thinking that he would soon see his grandfather and that whatever the situation, his grandfather would eventually reveal all to him. He started up towards the top of the mountain, to his eyes it did not seem particularly high and he felt that he would be across it in half an hour.

Much later, as the sun god's chariot slowly climbed the blue vault of heaven in the great wilderness beyond the Eastern Ocean behind him and galloped on above his head, Bogun

was still only halfway up, the mountain seemed to be growing of its own accord. He hurried on up, intending to overtake the mountain as it grew, until the sun inclined to the west and the fiery clouds reflected red on the mountain top as if the summit had dissolved into the red of the clouds. Bogun thought of the great god Kuafu and his pursuit of the sun. Kuafu had stridden across the Yellow River and the Wei River thinking that he would catch up with the sun in no time at all and had ignored the need to stop for water. This feeling had accompanied Kuafu until he collapsed, and the sun continued on its way as before. The light gradually faded and Bogun found a patch of soft grass where he lay down, intending, whatever happened, to sleep and revive his spirits before anything else. "If Kuafu could have slept for a bit like this, I guarantee he would have been able to catch the sun." It just so happened that it was the mid-summer and suitable for sleeping in the open, moreover, the stars of the Blue Dragon constellation that patrolled the southern skies must surely have heard him as he muttered in his dreams.

Bogu woke early next morning to discover, to his astonishment, that Qiongshan had not continued to grow but seemed to have

Kuafu Chases the Sun

2017
Xu Zengying (1977–)
Woodcut
Height 22 cm by width 30 cm

Legend has it that the giant Kuafu wanted to catch the sun so that heaven and earth would always be filled with warmth and sunlight. He chased the sun until it sank behind the hills but still did not catch up with it until, finally, he died of thirst. This legend embodies the attempts of our forefathers to transcend the bonds that limit life as well as their craving for immortality.

stopped when he did. Bogun was encouraged; since he had expended the whole of the previous day in reaching half-way, surely, at his present speed he would reach the summit today. He strode strongly upwards, faster than he had done the day before.

At sunset, Bogun looked up to see, not far away, a blue-black mountain peak. Looking back, he felt that he was still, more or less, only halfway. On this basis, however hard he struggled upwards, he was always at a distance from the summit that was neither near nor far. He had an ominous premonition: he would never reach the top of this mountain and would never get past it, and this was perhaps the significance of the name—Qiongshan, the mountain of no end, a mountain without limit.

ASKING THE WAY TO LINGSHAN

It looked as if his grandfather, the Yellow Emperor, really did not want to see him and Bogun, recalling what the Queen Mother of the West had said, turned back down the hill. The way down the hill was strangely easy and in no time at all Bogun was back at the place where he had parted from the dark bird. As he looked at Qiongshan for the last time, all he saw was a very ordinary rocky hill, with low shrubs growing up between patches of grass and rocks, a mountain whose summit was instantly visible.

The road to Lingshan was not hard. Crossing a great wilderness and traveling south until Venus appeared in the eastern heavens once more, Bogun's spirit arrived at the foot of a hill shrouded in mist and covered in verdant green trees where he saw ten shamans, darkly dressed, barefoot and with disordered hair, waiting to greet him. They were the ten shamans mentioned by the Queen Mother

Bronze Figure of a Standing Man
c. 1700–c. 1200 BC
Height of figure 180 cm, overall height 260.8 cm
Sanxingdui Museum, Sichuan Province

Excavated from the sacrificial mound at Sanxingdui. The figure wears a high crown on its head. The hands appear as if grasping empty space, the bare feet have ankle bracelets and stand on a square base made from a wild animal. The impression is one of a major figure of imposing appearance that is in touch with and reporting to heaven in the act of doing something. The bronze image is perhaps representative of shamans, able to travel in the space that lies between men and gods.

of the West: Wuxian, Wuji, Wupan, Wupeng, Wugu, Wuzhen, Wuli, Wudi, Wuxie and Wuluo. They formed a column, stretching elegantly up across the slope of the hill. At their head was Wuxian with a green snake in his right hand and a red one in his left. Bogun's spirit approached him and, seeking guidance, said:

"Great master, who travels between heaven and earth, who can find the rarest medicines from amongst grasses and flowers, who brought back to life the pitiful Yayu, slain by the god Erfu, who can divine the intentions of the gods from the movement of the stars and the flight of birds, who can understand the omens in the changes in tortoise shells and yarrow plants, tell me, please, what must an unfortunate soul, summoned by a god, then struck down and abandoned, think or do before he can bring peace to his stubborn spirit? I would dearly love to live once more, not for pleasure, but so I can make amends for the mistakes I have made. I have not completed what the gods ordered me to do, to control the floods that ravaged mankind and I brought fresh disaster upon them."

Wuxian then replied: "Young lord of the rivers, we have all heard what has befallen you. You underwent much hardship in attempting to control the waters by yourself and you took many risks in stealing the ever-growing soil, thereby unintentionally making a great mistake and suffering the extreme penalty. For a long time a soul, grieving at injustice and unable to escape has floated restlessly over this world of the west. Now that you have come to Lingshan we will do everything that we can to help you."

Wuxian went on: "Within each question that you have put, there lies an answer. Naturally, a question of error will contain an answer that will have difficulty in satisfying the questioner. Consequently, if we are to explain your questions, then we must first return to the very first of them. 'If the gods intend some fresh disaster, what can be the significance of the work that I am about to undertake?' If I'm not wrong, that was the first of the questions you asked and the last as well, isn't that so?"

"True, it was the question that I asked my father Luoming in the beginning, the final question that, as a living demi-god, I put to Zhurong was much the same," Bogun's soul replied.

"Then how is it that you believed that the fresh floods caused by the gods would be a repetition of previous disasters? Perhaps the supreme god was fed up with an endless cycle of disaster and reconstruction and seeing that this tinkering had wrought no change at all, may have hoped for the appearance of something new, otherwise why would he have dispatched a mere demi-god to control the waters? This was something that did not occur during the destruction caused by the first flood. You failed to consider the intentions of the gods carefully and took precipitate action," Wuxian said.

"I don't quite understand what you mean."

"The first flood was a product of the anger of the supreme god. At the time, although all-powerful, the very earliest father lacked experience. He gradually realized that the mankind he had created was, on its arrival, a less than perfect race. For the gods to seek human life that from the beginning is not corrupt is, like humans seeking to become gods, a vain hope. This new flood is just a reminder from the gods, not a disaster. Clearly, mankind is not aware of this reminder and has merely fled to the high ground where it ekes out a miserable existence. You should know that if the gods were bent on the destruction of mankind, what high ground exists where it could hide away?"

"So, when the gods instructed me to go control the waters, it was not just to control the waters?"

"That's so. As we shamans perceive it, the gods hoped that through you, a once again corrupt mankind could be brought to realize its fate and thenceforth begin a process of renewal, rather than lazily relying on yet another futile cleansing from the gods. The gods have wearied of the act of creation."

"It's only through you that I've come to understand all this. I really am stupid. To have only realized my mission after my life was over," said Bogun's spirit with a mournful sigh.

"There has never been an end to life. My child, life is diffused, it changes into wind and cloud, into plants and earth, into rocks as hard as iron, into the surging flow of water and the flickering flames of fire, but this diffusion is not an ending. In the end, a profoundly lived life is gathered together anew and takes form as a new life." So saying, the shaman Wuxian took a grain of grass from the shaman behind him, Wuji, and handed it to Bogun's spirit, "This is coix seed, eat it and return to the Weiyu Mountain and into your original body. There will be a new life that, on your behalf, will complete all that you have left undone."

Bogun obeyed Wuxian, ate the white fruit grain that resembled a string of pearls and returned to the Weiyu Mountain and re-entered the body that had lain sprawled on the ground. The body had not decomposed in the three years that had passed, it seemed like a piece of rock, its belly, though, grew larger by the day and was just like that of an expectant mother. When he learned of this, the Emperor Yao dispatched a god to Weiyu equipped with one of the famous sharp swords of Wu, who sliced open the rock-hard belly, whereupon a young, two-horned dragon leapt forth and soared into the sky. This was Yu the Great.

THE ARRIVAL OF YU THE GREAT

" The boundless traces of Yu marked out the nine provinces." (Meaning that wherever Yu the Great had been had become a part of the nine provinces—the territory of ancient China.) What follows is the story of how a god became a man. How, after being born from stone and burdened with a destiny unfulfilled by previous generations of gods and having wandered the earth and learned the ways of mountains, rivers, and the stars, he led the

Stone Relief Rubbing: *Yu the Great*

Eastern Han Dynasty
Wuliang Family Ancestral Hall, Jiaxiang County, Shandong Province
National Museum of China

In this portrait, Yu the Great is seen holding a plow (*si*) and wearing a rain hat while dressed in a wide-sleeved jacket and under-skirt. He is wearing shoes with square-shaped openings. Yu the Great led the taming of the floods, passing his own doorstep three times without returning home. He is thus regarded as a model of virtue amongst the ancients of China.

peoples scattered in a state of tribal barbarism, through trials and tribulations to control the disasters visited upon them by the gods. In undertaking this collective action, he rescued mankind from ignorance and corruption and established a state that was able to civilize its people and grew into Huaxia, ancient China, the nine provinces and eventually into the vast Chinese civilization of today.

Yu the Great in His Own Words I

I'm called Yu.

In those distant, far off days, people did not have names. Like birds and animals, mankind was a flock or herd. Men multiplied and spread but their only actual existence was first birth and then death, leaving not a trace behind. Only gods were different, the one from the other, each god had his own particular characteristic perpetual power and this power was enshrined in his name.

In the earliest pictograms you can clearly see that the character *yu* (禹) is formed by combining *jiu* (九), nine, and *chong* (虫), insect. In the past, there were scholars who concluded that I did not exist, that I was merely an animal totem worshipped by the Rong Tribe in the west. Later, the unfounded rumor that "Yu was an insect" was popular for a while and caused some famous authors to write novels in my defense. In fact, they had a misconception about me, a misconception based upon the ancient laws of nomenclature that has sunk without trace. In the space-time

continuum in which I was active, names were not a description of appearance or nature but a description of power, because mankind did not then have the knowledge to see through to the nature of a person. The only things that could be described accurately were the various powers and strengths that appeared between heaven and earth. The origin of the name "Yu" lies in the first battle I took part in. It is the act of fighting that wins you the right to a name.

I recall that it was the fight with Xiangliu, the nine-headed snake.

In the beginning, the Emperor Yao dispatched a god armed with one of the sharp swords of Wu to slice open the belly of my fossilized father Bogun, and a young dragon burst out. Carrying a yellow bear on its back, it flew slowly towards the northwest. That was the young me, bearing the departed soul

Album: *Ten Thousand Years of the Imperial Succession—Yu the Great and Qi* (from top to bottom)
Ming Dynasty
Qiu Ying
Ink and color on silk
Height 32.5 cm by width 32.6 cm
Palace Museum, Taibei

of my father, on my way to the Less-than-Whole Mountain to rest amongst familiar surroundings.

After I had buried my father, I wandered for a while in the northwest, visiting famous rivers and mountains. I met and received instructions from the shaman Wuxian who told me stories about my father Bogun and said: "Your father's failure was because he always tried to control the floods without the involvement of man. Your destiny is to enter within man." I then ate the magic plant on Lingshan, drank the sweet dew and through communing with the ten shamans, acquired the skills of all sorts of heavenly and earthly changes, so that I gradually grew and changed into a human and went to live amongst them.

After the death of my father, the gods expelled mankind for a while, as the land that had suffered drought and flood because of the ever-growing soil, had become the haunt of all sorts of evil spirits and monsters. I came across Xiangliu in a large patch of swamp. He had nine human heads but the body of a snake and could eat food from nine different hilltops at the same time. Wherever his tail touched the ground, it became a pool of bitter, evil-tasting water that killed the humans, birds and beasts that drank it. You can well imagine that there was no trace of life for a hundred *li* round his dwelling place.

I killed him, and the blood from his corpse stank and where it stained the ground, trees and plants withered and died. Three times I tried to bury him, and each time the earth collapsed as if corroded. I simply dug down and excavated a great pool and piled the spoil into a great platform facing south towards Kunlun. On the platform I piled fragrant pine and firewood and performed the ceremonies of sacrifice to the gods, asking the earth god to crush Xiangliu's corpse and praying to the rain god to send a storm to cleanse the surroundings of the stink of decomposition. Seeing the flames from afar, people rushed to see, their banners thronging the base of the platform, writing my name as "Yu" in the earthen paving, meaning the man who killed the nine-headed snake monster. I heard them shouting "Yu," the sound of the character for rain, perhaps meaning that I was also a man who could bring rain.

Yu the Great in His Own Words II: Hills, Rivers and Land

The people told me that this was the land of the western Qiang. Because of the floods and the snake they had only been able to live all together in caves on the top of the mountains, competing with wild animals for food, men and women mixed up, children knowing their mother but not their father, living the uncertain life of animals. I remembered what the shaman Wuxian had told me of the corruption, barbarism and promiscuity of mankind. The fury that I had felt in my heart was now replaced by a great pity and I decided to stay with them.

I made the western Qiang people take me to the top of a mountain close by and told them to cut down the trees at the top as fast as they could to make a path to the summit. Normally they nested in holes on the mountain and none of them had ever dared to visit the summit, believing that a place enveloped in mist was the dwelling place of the gods. Consequently, I was able to feel the excitement and unease as they jostled behind me on the difficult path to the top.

We struggled on for many days and eventually reached the summit. It so happened that it was dawn and a shining Venus hung in the scarlet east, the sky was a dark limpid blue, the birds were still silent and a few milk-white clouds floated amongst the dark hills. Behind me, the western Qiang people stood quietly, speechless as we gazed together at those most unforgettable red clouds of morning.

One of the western Qiang elders told me that, according to legend, one dawn, many years before, somebody had seen a great horned beast sitting on the top of the mountain with its head lowered, sipping at the waters below. Suddenly, in the twinkling of an eye, not a trace of the beast was to be seen. Later, after the sun had risen, the accumulated waters in the valleys below were seen to have utterly vanished. I knew that it was my father, Bogun. I was sad as I thought of his loneliness as he controlled the waters, how I wished I could have stood alongside him at the time.

After the sun had risen, standing on the mountaintop, it was possible to clearly make out the form of the earth. The waters surged to and fro in the valleys beneath our feet, and away in the distant plains, if you looked carefully, thin black lines snaked across the landscape, the ruins of the remaining dykes, whose general direction followed the mountain ridges as they rose and fell to the east and west, neither end visible to the eye. The massive mountains and flowing water divided the land between them. I asked the western Qiang people round me what was the most distant place that they had ever been to. They were extremely vague since they had no concept of near or far, like the seeds of plants they were blown hither and thither, born here and dying there.

I pointed out the distant mountain rages to them and asked whether they were willing to accompany me through this land of mountains and rivers. In the silence that followed, just one man, with a dark face and a great mouth like the muzzle of a horse, stood up and said that he was.

The two of us then bid farewell to the other western Qiang people. Before we left, I built a sacrificial altar at the very summit of the mountain that I had first climbed and told the western Qiang people that this mountain peak was called "Yue." It was the place on earth closest to the gods. If they wished to seek the help of the gods, they should come here regularly to build fires and make sacrifices. I demonstrated the ceremony of prayer to the gods for them and left with the man with the horse's muzzle following behind. I called him "Yao" which means "one who accompanies."

Yu the Great in His Own Words III: Making a Path through the Hills

My original plan was to follow a route along the terrain of the mountains and the flow of the rivers cutting a mountain path as I went. Man cannot soar the vast expanses of the heavens like a bird, nor can he swim the oceans like a fish, he must rely on paths to reach other places and other people. If there are paths, then, perhaps people may gain a sense of direction and can extract themselves from the mire of stupidity and ignorance. This is what I thought, having stood on the top of "Yue" and seen the hills and rivers winding their way into the distance together.

Gradually and as was to be expected people began to join us. At first, these scattered hill-dwellers had no understanding of what I was doing and watched, hidden, from a distance. When they realized that we were making a path out of the mountains and were making rapid progress (after all, I had the power of a god that an ordinary person did not possess), some people rushed over to help, lifting logs and clearing undergrowth and following us as we moved forward. This small band grew and grew. Each day, the noise of such a large group of people moving forward at lightning speed drowned out the thunderous roar of water in the hills and valleys. I gave each person a name and got Yao to draw up simple regulations and a system of rewards and punishments to govern common life. At the same time, work was allotted on the basis of

the individual's wishes and ability. There were a number of old people who knew the surrounding mountains well and they were asked to become guides and advisers. There were also some women who took on the making of fires and cooking. The men were divided into two groups, one group worked on road building and the other went hunting, with the two groups changing over every three days. Of course, the food obtained by hunting was often not enough for the number of people, so I went out and killed a boar or a deer for them to share. At night we sat round a fire singing.

The path grew longer day by day and everybody was in high spirits. I felt this was the first time that a group of mankind on earth had been driven forward by a common hope. I had not imposed this hope on them; on the contrary, I had never revealed the task of controlling the waters to them for fear that its sheer size would over-awe them. I thought that, as far as they were concerned, this hope was firstly about their unknown feelings and aspirations. Every day would produce a new situation on the road and new scenery as well. I even felt that I was leading mankind along a new path towards the gods, though this path was unlike the fragile but magnificent tower of Babel that reached heavenwards recorded in the biblical Old Testament.

Jade Sculpture: Yu the Great Taming the Floods

Qing Dynasty, Qianlong period
Height 224 cm by width 96 cm; height of base 60 cm, weight 5,000 kg
Palace Museum, Beijing

Made from dense blue/green jade. It is carved with mountain ranges and folds of hills, flowing waterfalls, ancient trees and blue pines, and deep caves. Amongst the cliffs and precipices teams of workers labor to bring the floods under control in the story of "Yu the Great taming the floods."

It was more a firm track that wound through mountain ranges.

I called the place from where we had started "Yue," later it was called Qianshan, now in Long County in Shaanxi Province. We followed the Qianshan Hill eastwards along the northern banks of the Wei River and reached Qishan where, later, the Zhou Dynasty started. The *Classic of Poetry* says: "The bitter herbs of fertile Zhou taste like honey." However, when we drove our road through the place, the plain that later nourished a great dynasty was still submerged by devastating floods. Intending to reach Jingshan from Qishan and carry on, we suddenly found that the mountain range that extended from west to east had been interrupted by a great river flowing from north to south, as if descending from heaven. At this point, the width of the river was limited by the rocks that hemmed it in on either side, so that its width was reduced from hundreds of meters to tens of meters. Once fast flowing and now suddenly obstructed by a mountain range, it erupted into a torrent of huge waves but flowed on nevertheless, flooding all around. Only later did I learn that this was the Yellow River and that the waters that we saw on our way were the result of the incessant flooding caused by the obstruction of the river on its way to the sea. But, at the time, because I had no grasp of the geography of the whole land, I could only secretly mark it all down and continue to lead everybody forward.

Following the Longmen Mountain that stood in the way of the Yellow River, we crossed the Leishou Mountain, the place where my ancestor, the Yellow Emperor, had mined copper to cast cauldrons of bronze, and reaching the end of the mountain range, turned northeast towards the Taiyue Mountains. We then followed the Dizhu Mountain south, crossed east over the Xicheng Mountain and followed the north bank of the Yellow River to Wangwushan. Following the Taihang Mountain ever eastwards, we crossed Hengshan and then followed the remainder of the Yanshan Range to Jieshishan on the shore of the Bohai Sea. It was here that we saw the sea at last, an unbounded blue, totally unlike the great pale muddy waters that we had seen so far. I also saw that from time to time, the sea spilled over on to the land and then withdrew, creating large expanses of uninhabited flood land.

Yu the Great in His Own Words IV: The Xia People

In this way, like some founding father, leading a band of here today gone tomorrow barbarians, I cut a road from the depths of the land to the ocean. Rather like the Yellow River we had seen along the way, new people were always joining and leaving us. I saw the river, obstructed by mountains, a vast obscurity created in a moment of thunderous frenzy; it was like the desperation that comes after the loss of a way out. Threshing around in mid-journey, the river seeks direction, but the closer it approaches its lower reaches, the broader and more placid it becomes because it has seen hope.

Mankind also needs hope. As the road progressed, I had seen with my own eyes how these barbarians, not too different from birds and beasts and living in fear and debauchery, had gradually become brand new. It was hope that had forged them anew and made them see the significance of their work, see how the road took shape, and taught them how, little by little, to reach out to the possibilities of the yet unknown. It was hope that had brought them to these distant parts and shown them the sea.

What next then? Floodwater still inundated the land, it was not enough just to have built a road, although, in the process and

through work and hope, I had had a vague glimpse of the fact that managing water and managing people were the same. It was not enough to continue as we were. It was not possible to carry on rushing about, and even if I could, the people would gradually become slack and idle. A new hope had to be found for them, one that felt different to the road, a more stable hope.

I wanted to find the source of the river. I already knew where it went but I wanted to know where it came from, only then could I tame it and return water to water and land to land. At the same time, I wanted to give this group of people a reason for existence.

Painting from *Illustrations to A Mirror for the Emperor (Dijian Tushuo)*
Bibliothèque nationale de France

This picture comes from the *Jieqi Qiuyan* chapter of *Illustrations to A Mirror for the Emperor* that describes how Yu the Great hung out a variety of instruments which people might sound to give notice of raising issues on various subjects.

A Mirror for the Emperor was personally compiled by Cabinet Grand Secretary Zhang Juzheng (1525–1582) as a book of instruction for the infant Emperor Wanli (1563–1620), then barely ten years old. It is made up of a number of stories, each story with a matching illustration. The book is divided into two sections; the first, Fragrant Rules of the Sages, describes the efforts and achievements of historical emperors in ruling the empire and the second, the Errors of Stupidity analyses the perverse decisions and actions of previous emperors.

Ming Dynasty Embroidery of a *Xiezhi*

Gaotao is regarded as the ancestor of Chinese traditional legal officials. According to legend, Gaotao kept a mythological animal that was able to distinguish between truth and falsehood, crooked and straight and helped him reach judgement. *Xiezhi* is a symbol of traditional Chinese law and has been revered over many dynasties. Up until the Qing Dynasty, imperial censors and investigating officials charged with the oversight of the legal system all wore gowns embroidered with a *xiezhi* design.

I wanted to establish a nation, a place of everlasting hope. I called it "Xia." I envisaged that the character would take the form of a person with two hands and two feet at work and would be pronounced like the character *xia*—"underneath." It would mean that this nation was the projection on earth below of the heavenly nation above.

They all obeyed me and looked on me as a god, the men and women, the old people and even the children slowly and ceaselessly born on the way. They were overjoyed when they heard that they were to have their own nation. I taught them the concept of respect, to serve as an example in all things and to strive and live as oneself. I also taught them simplicity in eating and clothing, to serve and respect gods and ghosts, and as to matters between men and women, to put mutual joy first and if one party was no longer willing, then to separate without entanglement; children were to be handed over to the wise elders to be raised and educated in common.

Outside my tent I hung a bell (*zhong*), a drum (*gu*), a chime (*qing*), another larger bell (*duo*), and a hand drum (*tao*), for the use of all, announcing widely that those who wished to approach me on matters of morality should strike the drum, on justice they should strike the bell, those who had matters to discuss should ring the other larger bell, those with anxieties should strike the chime and those with accusations should rattle the hand drum.

In this place, close to the sea, the waters raged, it was no place to live safely or to work happily. Once more, I led them, the earliest Xia people, back along the road that we had built. When we reached the area of Yangcheng of Mount Song, a great hill stood facing the water with its back to the mountains, the terrain was high but level and I stopped the Xia people and told them of my original ambition to bring the floods under control. To achieve this I needed to find the source of the river. Those who had the will could continue to follow me, but those who no longer wished to be always on the move, particularly women, children, the old and the sick, could settle here in my name and I would return once I had finished the task of controlling the floods. I left behind Gaotao, who was versed in law, to govern and Ji, skilled in agriculture, to teach the people how to plant and cultivate the five cereals and build houses and terraced fields against the hill, so that even if the floods returned, they could swiftly withdraw to the hills and there would be no anxiety over food and clothing. Having handed over all this, I left with my long-time attendant Yao and a few sturdy and energetic young men and continued upstream.

Yu the Great in His Own Words V: Managing the Water and Spreading the Soil

In fact, we did not reach the source of the river. We reached Jishishan, the mountains of stone in Qinghai and stopped there. Here, we followed the riverbed and found a small stream trickling from between the rocks and flowing sluggishly round and round. The mountain was magnificent, filled with precious metals and covered with strange and wonderful flowers and fruit. We thought, at the time, that this was the mountain from which the river flowed. Besides, the terrain became higher and higher as you traveled from east to west and having traced the river this far, and since it was already thin and weak and incapable of threatening a flood, there seemed no point in going any further.

Setting out from Jishishan we once more followed the stream downwards. By now, I knew the river well, its multitude of tributaries, its winding course, and its low water and flood times. This naturally formed a riverbed that had never been managed or controlled. The depths and shallows, widths and narrows, were all formed by the desires of the river and silt itself. What we had to do was to clean and dredge the riverbed, particularly where it was silted up in midstream. It had

Rock Rubbing: *The Shimen Ode* (detail)
Eastern Han Dynasty, 2nd Year of Jianhe (148)
Hanzhong City Museum, Shaanxi Province

This inscription is one of the most famous examples in China of a Han inscription and a fine example of Han clerical script. It is part of the ode "Yu bores through the dragon gate," a response to the legend of Yu the Great taming the floods and boring through Longmen, the dragon gate. The writer honors the Metropolitan Commandant, Yang Mengwen, for following in the footsteps of Yu the Great by tunneling through Shimen, the stone gate.

The ode is carved in vertical oblongs of height 261 cm and width 205 cm, with 20 lines and 30 or 31 characters to a line, totaling 655 characters altogether. With its majestic air and unconstrained individualism, the inscription is regarded as the progenitor and model for cursive clerical script. It is both neat and regular, yet rich in change and full of feeling and not confined to a single form.

to be widened and deepened and the dredged silt and soil used to build high dykes, thereby improving the flow between the river and its minor tributaries and lakes and keeping the main river on a fixed course. High dykes had also to be built along the other meandering flows of water to form lakes and ponds as reservoirs for the river and to fill in and raise the surrounding low-lying ground and make it habitable and suitable for farming.

After a long time we reached Longmen once more, where the river flooded the most.

I had already thought that "where the mountain blocks the river, bore through it" would be the only way of solving the flooding here caused by backed up water. However, there had been the unremitting toil of dredging the rivers and building the dykes and even if the manpower was available the task of driving through a mountain was beyond the strength of man. I was afraid that I would have to make use of my supernatural powers.

I thought of my father, Bogun, who had attempted over the years to control the floods with his own supernatural powers, who, in the end, had died and whose achievements had come to naught. I had always followed the instructions of the shaman, Wuxian, "enter into man;" managing water and managing man is the same thing. Before controlling the floods I had established the Xia people and brought these scattered, shiftless people together and given them a hope, using that hope to complete the work of controlling the waters. But now I would probably have to use a strength that no man possessed, gods and teachers forgive me.

In the middle of the night, I turned myself into a huge yellow bear, standing across the river with a foot on either bank and little by little, using my paws, attacking the hard rock face and splitting in two the great mountain that stood in the river's way, allowing the river water to pour through this door-like cleft between two cliffs, as if into a deep pot. Later, people called the mountain on the west bank, Longmen, dragon's gate, and the one on the east, Hukou, the pot mouth.

That night, as I waded through the water into the opened mountain, I discovered that a ravine in the left wall of the mountain twisted away into the remote depths with a faint light at the very end. I lit a torch and went to investigate. As I entered, a wild boar suddenly scuttled out of the grass to one side with a great luminescent pearl in its mouth, illuminating all around and a great gray dog came barking and showing the way. I knew at once that there were gods and spirits here. We traveled like this along the ravine for about ten *li*. Beneath the light of the luminescent pearl, I could not quite make out whether it was day or night. Suddenly I saw the boar and the dog that were leading me turn into human figures clad in black. I also saw a god with the body of a snake and the face of a man sitting upright on a rock with eight attendants on either side behind him, the sleeves of their garments floating lightly in the air. I thought of someone and moved forward to pay my respects, asking: "I have heard that Huaxu gave birth to a sacred son. I do not know whether that is your honored self or not?" He nodded and said: "Huaxu was the goddess of the nine rivers, I am that son." I knew then that he was Fuxi. Fuxi called me forward and presented me with a book in which were written the directions of all the mountains and rivers of the world and a jade writing slip of a length of one *chi* and two *cun* (15.7 inches) with which to measure the world at any time. I knew then that the Emperor of Heaven had seen all that I had done, and approved.

From the book I learned that apart from the great river of the north (the Yellow River), there was another large river in the south (the Yangtze). The general layout of terrain can be seen as two systems of rivers, north and south. In the north, the system runs from Sanweishan and Jishishan, along the line of the sunless side of the Zhongnan Mountains, east to Taihua Range, across the river to the mountains of Leishou, Xicheng, Wangwushan and Taihang and then north to Hengshan and east to Saiyuan and Korean peninsula. I had

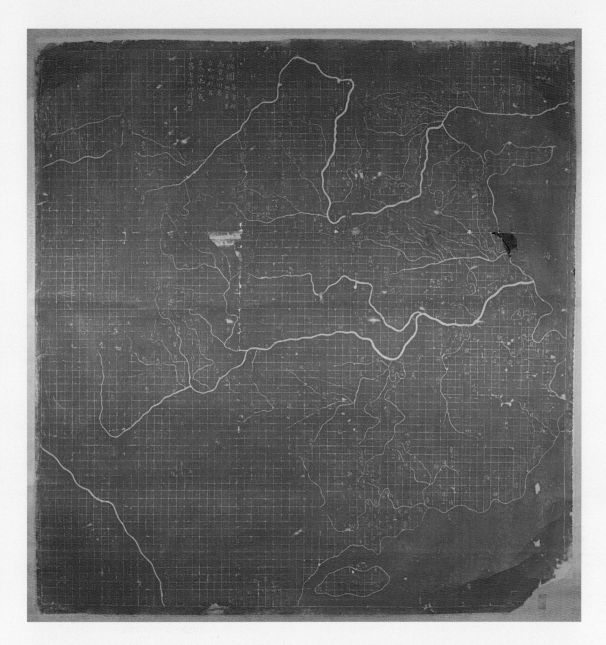

Map of the Tracks of Yu the Great (*Yuji Tu*)

Song Dynasty
Height 79 cm by width 78 cm
National Library of China

This is a rubbing from a stone tablet of a map of China made in the 7th year of Fuchang of the State of Qi (1136). The stone tablet is currently preserved in the Forest of Steles in Xi'an. As far as can be made out, the map preserves some of the Tang Dynasty place names which may have been based on a reduction of the nine provinces in the *Yu Gong* section of the "Map of China and Barbarians within the Seas (*Hainei Huayi Tu*)" and consequently known as "Map of the Tracks of Yu the Great." According to legend, when Yu the Great brought the floods under control he divided the world into nine provinces which then became a name for the known world. The map is aligned along a north/south axis and displays over 500 place names presenting a picture of the whole of China at the time of the Song Dynasty. River and water systems are particularly well detailed and include the names of nearly 80 lakes and rivers. The presentation of the courses of the Yellow and Yangtze rivers is very close to that of the maps of today. The outline of the coast is also very accurate. This map is a fine example of the cartographical skills of the Song Dynasty and occupies an important position in the history of Chinese cartography.

already traveled along this line. In the south, the system runs from Minshan and Bozhong, along the sunlit aspect of the terrain eastwards to the Taihua Range including Shangshan, Xiong'ershan, Waifangshan and Tongboshan. Then from the area of Peiweishan it turns south across the great river and the Han River, taking in Wudangshan and Jingshan and on to Hengyang and then following the Wuling range east to the area of Fujian. All this was the land that I had yet to cover.

The flow of rivers and the ranges of mountains go to make up terrain or the lie of the land. Taken overall, laterally this runs from east to west and vertically from north to south.

Leaving aside the Yellow River and the Yangtze, the north contains the Wei and Luo rivers that flow into the Yellow River; with the Ji and Huai rivers that flow into the sea on their own in the center. In the south, there is the Han River that flow into the Yangtze. Successive control of all seven of these rivers would eliminate flooding throughout

the land. How difficult a task this was! But once having met Fuxi, I felt that the time of greatest difficulty was now past.

Yu the Great in His Own Words VI: As the Will of the Gods Would Have It

All the gods were willing to help me.

There was Yaoji, for example, who possessed all kinds of mysterious powers and with whom I used to play when I was a child at Lingshan. Later, she had been returning from a tour of the Eastern Ocean and had been captivated by the beauty of the jagged mountains and tree-clad hills and valleys of Wushan and had stayed there. When I had been about to bore through the Three Gorges, the task had been so immense that it was beyond me. Suddenly there was a great storm that shook the cliffs and sent rocks flying. Hearing that she was nearby I sought her advice. She was pleased to see her childhood companion and we sat together

The Qianlong Emperor on a Tour of Inspection of the South (detail of the fourth scroll)

Qing Dynasty
Xu Yang (dates of birth and death unknown)
Ink and color on paper
Height 68.6 cm by length 1096.17 cm
Metropolitan Museum of Art, New York

This scroll depicts the Emperor Qianlong's (1711–1799) first visit of inspection to the south in the 16th year of his reign (1751). There are twelve scrolls in this set. The fourth scroll of the set shows Qianlong, having crossed the Yellow River, inspecting the same day and the day after, the strategically important engineering works at the confluence of the four waterway systems of the Huai and Yellow rivers, the Grand Canal, and the Hongze Lake. This work realistically depicts the natural aspects of the confluence of the two rivers as well as the dykes on the Huai River and demonstrates the unalterable fact that in 1770 the Yellow River entered the sea through the mouth of the Huai River. The majority of present-day scholars rely on local gazetteers, gazeteers of rivers and canals and archaeological excavation of the original course of the Yellow River for their study of the Yellow River and most of them have not come across the "Yellow/Huai Confluence." However, the painters of the Ruyi Guan, the imperial palace department responsible to the emperor for the study and display of the results of foreign technology, recorded this natural landscape, proof that historically the Yellow River entered the sea by way of the mouth of the Huai River.

The above picture depicts the confluence of the Yellow River and the Huai River. The Huai River is a dark blue/green and the Yellow River is yellow. When the Emperor Qianlong saw the confluence of the two rivers he pointed at this wonder and enquired about it from an official wearing the official yellow riding jacket (see the detail on pages 174–175).

talking all day. I told her of the work that I had been doing with mankind these last few years. For her part, she told me of the skills that she had learned from the immortals and taught me the magic art of summoning spirits and commanding demons. She also gave me a book that would prevent flood and tempest and ordered her assistant gods, Kuangzhang, Yuyu, Huangmo, Dayi, Gengchen and Tonglu to help me control the floods, break rocks and dredge and dam the channels. She told me to bring them back to the Kunlun Mountain

with me once the task was finished. I laughed and said that there was no place on Kunlun for me. I had already become an ordinary mortal. She understood and said no more.

Gengchen, Tonglu and the other gods really did help me a great deal. When controlling the waters of the Huai River I had more than once tried to find its source in the Tongboshan but it was always howling with wind and thunder, the rocks shrieking and the trees moaning, as if haunted by evil spirits, so that it was nigh impossible to begin the task of controlling the waters. I called on the mountain and earth gods and summoned the *kui* dragon only to discover that the water spirit Wuzhiqi was hidden away in the depths of the Huai River. He had the form of an ape with a high forhead and a flat nose, a dark body and white head, golden eyes and bloody fangs and a neck that could stretch for a hundred *chi*. He took in and out huge volumes of water and mist like an enormous elephant. He was quick and nimble and understood the speech of men, answering glibly with his own brand of mischievous reason. I sent Tonglu to catch him but he could not, nor could Wumuyou. Eventually it was Gengchen who took on the task and finally brought him under control, chaining him by the neck with great fetters of iron and putting a golden bell in his nose and imprisoning him beneath the Gui Hills in Huaiyin so that the Huai River was brought under control and flowed peacefully to the sea.

I was thirty years old, they all said I should have a family, the girls liked me but my heart only had room for the task of controlling the floods. It was as if the water had become my lover, I knew her pleasure and anger, sorrow and joy, her devious rhythms, her elegance and her arbitrary moods. I watched the earth's waters gathering slowly in the channels that now led to the ocean and felt a great peace. So much water flowed towards the sea and yet the sea did not overflow. I had met so many girls and not one had raised waves in my heart.

Until I met her.

I met her on a hill in the south. That day, I had lost my way surveying the water by myself and walked at least nineteen kilometers. As I crossed a path through dense forest, a prickly white rose descended from the sky, a pure flower, heavily scented and of a strange beauty and I began to feel

as if there was a girl beside me. She knew of all my questions about men and gods and understood my perplexities about the unattainable aims of my travels. Distracted in mind and spirit I walked on until I saw a large yellow butterfly hovering over a patch of purple asters, the illusion suddenly sank away like a ship and she stood before me. She led me deep into the hills as the glowworms flickered after us.

I spent four days in the hills with her and after so many years of toiling amongst humanity, I experienced the joys of the gods once more.

I took her to meet my clan and told them that I was married. They asked where she came from; I had forgotten the name of her hill and just called it Tushan. Tu means road and she of the Tushan clan was my road through the labyrinth.

However, the task of controlling the floods was still unfinished. I settled her down and continued my journeys, the remote distance of hills and valleys adding naturally to our relationship. Ten months later I learned that I had a son. The messenger had brought with him a stone on which were inscribed the

The Qianlong Emperor on a Tour of Inspection of the South **(detail of the fourth scroll)**
The above picture depicts the closing of the watergate in the Huai River dyke. Bundles of reeds are piled on top of the dyke to close the gap in the dyke.

words "Oh, I await you." The son I had yet to meet, I called "Qi." "Qi" means the sight of the morning star in the east, much as I had met her in the hills of the south.

Yu the Great in His Own Words VII: A Condemnation of Offensive War and Setting up the Tripod Cauldrons

I had originally thought that with the inspiration of the Emperor of Heaven, the help of the gods and the completion of the task of controlling the floods within sight, I would satisfy the desires of my father and be able to swiftly return to my wife and settle down together. But later events, one upon another, were beyond my anticipation.

First was war with the tribes of the Three Miao. The Miao were an ancient tribe, long

Stone Relief: *Recovering the Tripod Cauldrons from the Sishui River*

Pottery
Late Western Han Dynasty
Height 34 cm by width 112 cm
Henan Museum

Excavated in 1985 from No. 24 Han tomb at Fanji in Xinye County, Nanyang City, Henan Province. According to legend, the nine tripod cauldrons cast by Yu the Great were handed down to the Xia (2100–1600 BC), Shang and Zhou dynasties. However, probably because of the confusion caused by warfare, after three dynasties, they were lost in the waters of the Sishui River. When Emperor Qin Shihuang was passing through Pengcheng after his unification of China he noticed the nine tripod cauldrons floating in the Sishui River and dispatched several thousand men to salvage them, but without success.

The stone relief displays the historical story of Emperor Qin Shihuang's attempt to recover the nine tripod cauldrons. There are no empty spaces on the brick, which gives an impression of solidity. The scene is deftly portrayed with great emphasis on movement.

versed in the magic arts, which lived between Dongting and the great marsh of Pengze in the area of what is now Hengshan and Qishan in Hebei and Hunan provinces. Although, in the long term, control of the floods benefited the lives of all the people who lived in the Yangtze River basin, in the short term it damaged the vital interests of the Three Miao people. As the road was opened, regions that hitherto had been closed off and self-sufficient were suddenly opened to an influx of strangers; as the channels between rivers, lakes and marshes were dredged, the water level rose and Dongting and Pengze were suddenly flooded, drowning many aboriginal villagers; on top of this there were obstacles to communication and the teams of Xia clan flood workers that I sent were massacred by the Three Miao. That summer, the waters suddenly froze, the earth quaked open and often, at dusk the sun once more leaped across the sky and the day was as lacquer-dark as night, blood-red rain fell for three days and three nights, temples of sacrifice to ancestors and gods were plastered with patterns of dragons, dogs howled in the streets and the grain crops were destroyed. The Emperor of Heaven thereupon called me to the Black Palace, bestowed a jade symbol of office upon me and ordered me to lead men and gods in a punitive expedition against the Three Miao.

This was the first war that I had started. It was completely different to the wars against Xiangliu or Wuzhiqi that I had experienced in the past. In those wars against demons and ghosts, I knew very clearly that I was waging war against pure evil in defense of mankind. This war against the Three Miao, however, was between one group of mankind and another. I saw men and women, young and old, alike in body to my Xia clan, meeting their death on the battlefield. I saw men who looked like each other slaughtering each other and even though I was upholding the so-called will of heaven, I still found it difficult to bear. The first time, I did not know where absolute virtue and righteousness lay and I

had doubts about my conduct and actions. However, having reached this point, I had to carry on.

War is like an epidemic, once it appears it then spreads. Massacre follows upon massacre. Having once suppressed the Three Miao with the strength of blood and iron, I then launched a war against Youhushi and Fangfengshi, again in the name of the will of heaven.

I felt that I was rapidly becoming old. It was the succession of victorious wars that was ageing me, not the endless toil of controlling the waters.

The war was at last over and the disastrous floods brought under control. People everywhere called me "King." I ordered them to gather up all the metal implements in the world, the iron tools used for boring out rivers and splitting open mountains that had become weapons of metal used for cutting and stabbing flesh, and offer them all up on mount Jingshan in imitation of the act of my ancestor, the Yellow Emperor. These weapons would be thrown into a great fire and transformed into a thick river of steel from which would be cast nine great tripod cauldrons that would require the strength of

ninety thousand men to move.

I ordered that a record of the strange and wonderful things that we had encountered throughout the length and breadth of the land as we brought the floods under control, and the knowledge of the stars we had acquired through countless sleepless nights should all be incised on these cauldrons. Yao would remind me of the places that I had forgotten. He had followed me from the very beginning, he spoke the languages of the animals and of foreign tribes and had noted down all the strange things we had come across. He was the man who had helped me most and I bestowed on him the title of "Yi," the benefactor. Later, people all referred to him respectfully as Boyi.

I also ordered that the story of the two of us and of our love and dreams should be inscribed on the cauldrons in a place that people would not notice.

There was no inscription about war, or about all the suffering, or the evils and sacrifice. I knew that the life of these cauldrons would last longer than those of all of us and that the clans of the future would only need to distinguish the wonderful events from the rest.

EPILOGUE

The voice of Yu the Great,

Resounded amongst mountain and river.

Ancient myths spread afar,

And civilization reached all.

All peoples became one,

And a nation was born.

A glorious new chapter in history,

Opening along the Yangtze and Yellow rivers.

DATES OF THE CHINESE DYNASTIES

Xia Dynasty（夏）...2100–1600 BC

Shang Dynasty（商）...1600–1046 BC

Zhou Dynasty（周）..1046–256 BC

    Western Zhou Dynasty（西周）.................................1046–771 BC

    Eastern Zhou Dynasty（东周）.................................770–256 BC

        Spring and Autumn Period（春秋）....................770–476 BC

        Warring States Period（战国）........................475–221 BC

Qin Dynasty（秦）..221–206 BC

Han Dynasty（汉）...206 BC–AD 220

    Western Han Dynasty（西汉）.................................206 BC–AD 25

    Eastern Han Dynasty（东汉）.................................25–220

Three Kingdoms（三国）...220–280

    Wei（魏）..220–265

    Shu Han（蜀）...221–263

    Wu（吴）...222–280

Jin Dynasty（晋）..265–420

    Western Jin Dynasty（西晋）...................................265–316

    Eastern Jin Dynasty（东晋）...................................317–420

Northern and Southern Dynasties（南北朝）.....................420–589

    Southern Dynasties（南朝）....................................420–589

    Liang Dynasty（梁）...502–557

    Northern Dynasties（北朝）....................................439–581

Sui Dynasty（隋）..581–618

Tang Dynasty（唐）...618–907

Five Dynasties and Ten Kingdoms（五代十国）..............907–960

    Five Dynasties（五代）...907–960

    Ten Kingdoms（十国）..902–979

Song Dynasty（宋）...960–1279

    Northern Song Dynasty（北宋）..............................960–1127

    Southern Song Dynasty（南宋）.............................1127–1279

Liao Dynasty（辽）..916–1125

Jin Dynasty（金）..1115–1234

Xixia Dynasty (or Tangut)（西夏）.....................................1038–1227

Yuan Dynasty（元）...1279–1368

Ming Dynasty（明）...1368–1644

Qing Dynasty（清）...1644–1911